Deanne Anders was reading romance while her friends were still reading Nancy Drew, and she knew she'd hit the jackpot when she found a shelf of Harlequin Presents in her local library. Years later she discovered the fun of writing her own. Deanne lives in Florida, with her husband and their spoiled Pomeranian. During the day she works as a nursing supervisor. With her love of everything medical and romance, writing for Mills & Boon Medical Romance is a dream come true.

Also by Deanne Anders

From Midwife to Mummy
The Surgeon's Baby Bombshell
Stolen Kiss with the Single Mum
Sarah and the Single Dad

Discover more at millsandboon.co.uk.

DECEMBER REUNION IN CENTRAL PARK

DEANNE ANDERS

MILLS & BOON

First published in Great Britain 2021
by Mills & Boon, an imprint of HarperCollins*Publishers* Ltd,
1 London Bridge Street, London, SE1 9GF

www.harpercollins.co.uk

HarperCollins*Publishers*
1st Floor, Watermarque Building,
Ringsend Road, Dublin 4, Ireland

Large Print edition 2022

December Reunion in Central Park
© 2021 Harlequin Enterprises ULC

Special thanks and acknowledgement are given to
Deanne Anders for her contribution to
The Christmas Project miniseries.

ISBN: 978-0-263-29375-3

04/22

MIX
Paper from
responsible sources
FSC
www.fsc.org
FSC™ C007454

This book is produced from independently certified
FSC™ paper to ensure responsible forest management.
For more information visit www.harpercollins.co.uk/green.

Printed and Bound in the UK using 100% Renewable
Electricity at CPI Group (UK) Ltd, Croydon, CR0 4YY

This book is dedicated to
boss extraordinaire, Debbie Charlton,
and the best of co-workers, Stefanie Porche.
I will always be appreciative
of your support.

CHAPTER ONE

ENDLESS CLOUDS FLOATED by as Dr. Scott Thomas looked outside the plane that was taking him home. Home? Was it still home? Despite how hard the last year and a half had been, he'd come to think of London as home. But still something was missing. No, make that someone. His home hadn't felt the same since he and Felicity had dashed off to New York to be with her parents. He'd not known at the time that she wouldn't be coming back with him.

He punched the pillow he'd been given earlier and tried to reposition himself. The transatlantic flight was going to be rough on him the next day if he didn't get some rest, and he wanted to be at his best when he arrived to work the next day. The chance to help another hospital set up a specialty cardiac unit like the one at his own hospital, the Royal Kensington Hospital, was something that excited him, and it had been a while since he'd been really excited about anything.

Nothing could have surprised him more than to be offered this chance to be part of The Kensington Project, and while a part of him had been only too happy to return to New York, another part of him worried about what he might find when he finally made it to his hometown.

His parents, of course, were thrilled with the opportunity to see him, especially since he'd be remaining in New York till after the holidays. And then there was Felicity. Would she be happy to see him? Or would she wish him on his way, as she had the last time he'd seen her? Where exactly had they gone wrong?

"Is there anything I can get you?" A soft voice came from beside him.

Looking up, he saw that one of the flight attendants was standing over him. She'd spoken to him earlier in the flight, offering him a blanket and pillow.

"No, I'm fine, but thank you," he said. It had been pretty apparent that she wanted to start a conversation with him, though he had been careful not to encourage her.

"You sure?" she asked. "You seem a bit… distracted."

Her badge said her name was Kristen, and she made an attractive picture in her trim navy suit with her honey-blond hair and golden sun-touched skin that hinted of time spent in much warmer climates than those with which he was familiar. And just like every woman he had met in the last eighteen months, he wasn't even tempted to ask her for her full name.

"May I?" she asked as her hand indicated the empty seat next to his.

"Sure," he said as he repositioned himself more upright in his own seat.

"I take it from your accent that you're from the States. So am I. Are you headed home?" she asked.

There was that word again. *Home.* It had never seemed as complicated as it had in the last few months.

"I grew up in New York, but I work in London now," he said. "Is New York your home?"

"It is right now," she said. "I move around a lot. So, married? Single?" she asked with a smile that could be dangerously sexy, he was sure, but still he felt nothing.

What would it take to make him feel that heart-pounding adrenaline-buzz attraction again? He feared there was only one smile that would ever get that kind of response from him.

He realized she was staring at him and still waiting for his answer. "I'm single. I mean… I'm not married."

"A girlfriend, then?" she asked him.

The conversation was making him a bit uncomfortable, but he knew it wasn't her fault.

"It's complicated," he said, hoping that this would end her interrogation.

"Isn't love always complicated?" She gave him another smile and moved to get up. Apparently she had heard all she needed to hear. "Maybe we'll meet again sometime and things won't be complicated."

He watched as she walked back and joined the other attendants at the front of the plane, then adjusted his pillow once more. Love, complicated? It had never seemed to be that way for his parents, but the last few months had proved to him that emotions made people, even people you thought you really knew, unpredictable.

He stretched his seat back and closed his eyes. Immediately his mind got caught up in thoughts of complicated love and memories that seemed to be burned into his brain on a movie reel that he had replayed over and over for the last eighteen months.

It always opened up the same way...

A perfect moonlit night at that little sidewalk café that was her favorite; laughter while they sipped wine and talked about their day. Then they'd walk through the English garden in the park just blocks from his London home.

He could almost smell the sweet scent of the hydrangea blooms as they walked hand in hand and talked of everything and nothing, never tiring of hearing what the other had to say. It was always as if they were two strangers meeting for the first time and wanting to know everything about the other, instead of two people who had grown up together from childhood.

And even when silence fell between the two of them, there was no sign of awkwardness. They'd continued their walk until they stopped to share a kiss that seemed to change everything—a change they embraced as one kiss led to another until they were both racing to his place, together.

If only he could stop the memories there...

Scenes of kisses and touches played over in his mind: a vision of her stripped bare for him; the sight of her stretched out in his bed; the feel of her in his arms as they lay sated from their lovemaking.

He twisted in his seat and tried to will his mind to stop there. To leave him with that last happy memory of brushing long blond hair from sleepy blue eyes and wishing her a good night as they fell into slumber together, wrapped around each other for the first time.

But, no, there was no happy ending for the movie his mind insisted on playing for him each night as he tried to sleep.

There was always the insistent ringing of a phone, and the words his father had choked out as he gave Scott the news that had brought his life to a screeching halt— Scott's best friend, and Fliss's brother, was *dying*. Suicide, his father had said, though Scott refused to believe that this was possible, arguing with his father that he had to be mistaken as his father pleaded for him to find Fliss and break the news to her in person so she *wouldn't* be alone.

He'd looked down at the woman lying in his bed, the one he was falling in love with, and had known instinctively that nothing would ever be the same.

Finally the last scene replayed itself.

In his arms, he held his lover and friend,

whose tears and sobs broke what was left of his heart after the loss of his friend.

Scott's eyes flew open. Looking around the plane, he was glad to see he hadn't drawn anyone's attention. He looked at his watch. He had three more hours before they landed at JFK and there was no way he was going to sleep now. Dragging out his laptop, he dug into the reports he'd been given on Brooklyn Heights Hospital's new cardiac unit. He might be tired when he showed up the next day, but at least he'd be up to date and ready to get to work.

It had finally happened. She'd lost her mind. That was the only excuse she had for why she was standing in the middle of the emergency-room hallway, staring at the back of some man's head. It had been bound to happen at some point. She couldn't continue to work seven days a week, twelve to sixteen hours a day, without this happening. Of course, she could see why this man had gotten her attention. That thick head of dark chocolate-brown hair in that specific close-cropped cut was like a magnet for her eyes—eyes that were apparently tired from lack of sleep, because no matter what they were telling her, that man couldn't be Scott.

She looked around the hallway. It was the same New York City crowded hallway where she had spent most of her hours in the last year. It was definitely not the Royal Kensington Hospital elite cardiac unit in London, where Scott could be found.

Clenching her hands, she felt the vial of medication in her hand. She had to get back to her patient. She didn't have time for this nonsense. There had to be plenty of men that could resemble Scott from the back.

She two-stepped it down the hallway, dodging stretchers and wheelchairs, but a sense of unease still followed her back to her patient's room. It had been a strange experience to react to a man that way, especially when she could barely see his profile.

Entering the room, she noted that the young woman's heart rate was still tachycardia and had gone from running in the one-eighties to the two-hundreds now.

"It's going to be okay, Jenny," Felicity said to the young woman who was even more pale and diaphoretic than she had been when she first arrived.

"The vagal maneuver hasn't helped?" she asked the emergency-room doctor.

"No. Go ahead and draw up the adenosine," he said.

Drawing up the medication, she wiped down the IV port and then attached the syringe. "Has Dr. Campbell explained how adenosine works?"

"He said it should make my heart slow down, but also that I might feel some chest pain and dizziness." Jenny's bright green eyes shone with a look of panic that Felicity was used to seeing in the emergency room.

"I'll be right here with you," Felicity said as she took Jenny's hand into her free one, preparing to inject the medication into the IV line.

"Are you ready?" she asked her patient,

then looked over at the doctor who nodded his head for her to push the medication that would basically stop Jenny's heart before it returned into a normal rhythm.

She squeezed the young woman's hand and pushed the medication. Everyone's attention went to the monitor above the bed as the cardiac rhythm began to slow until there was a pause.

"Oh," the young woman said as she clutched both of their hands to her chest, bringing Felicity's attention back to her. Pain and panic filled the woman's eyes.

"It's okay. The worst is over, I promise. Just hang on a few more seconds." Felicity looked back up at the monitor to see that the heart rate was gradually slowing to a normal sinus rhythm. "Is it better now?"

Jenny nodded her head, but Felicity could tell that she hadn't totally recovered. At least some of the young woman's color was returning now. "Can I get you something?"

"No, I'm better now." The young woman's voice trembled, but she let go of Felicity's hand and closed her eyes. "I'm just going to rest a minute."

"I'll be right here if you need anything," Felicity said as the rest of the staff began to leave the room. She would remain in the room with her patient until she was assured the young woman was stable and then have her transferred to the cardiac floor for observation and more testing to find the cause behind her tachycardia.

She was turning to get her patient a blanket when her eyes came to a stop as she saw the man from earlier standing outside the glass doors of the trauma room. Who was he, and why did he have to be here in her ER, upsetting her now when she needed to be concentrating on her patient?

Yes, the man was at least as tall as Scott and they did share the same basic build that included a pair of very wide shoulders. And, yes, this man did have the exact same haircut that Scott had always favored, but it was more than that. Something deep down inside her told her she knew him.

Turn around. Let me see your face.

Her heart was beating as fast as her patient's had earlier.

For a moment she let herself imagine that it was Scott. That he had come back to see her. But how would he have known where to find her? Unlike the years when they had been separated by colleges in different states, there had been no late-night calls that went on for hours, nor had there been the funny texts that they had shared for years as they checked up on each other. Felicity had known they needed a clean break. Ignoring his calls and texts had added more heartache to her life, but she would never have survived hearing about Scott's life without her.

"Are you okay?" Dr. Campbell asked as he came to a stop at the door, blocking her view. For a moment she thought the doctor was talking to her patient before she realized he was speaking to her.

"Yes, we're good. I'll let you know if there are any changes in her rhythm." She had to get herself together. She had a job to do and it did not include daydreaming.

She took a blanket off the shelf beside the stretcher and covered the young woman before allowing herself to walk over to the doorway. If Scott's doppelgänger had ever actually existed, he was gone now. It was official. She was losing her mind.

Checking her patient's vital signs again, she made herself concentrate on getting her charting done. There were only a couple of hours left in her shift and then she had to go to the new unit and check on progress there.

"Hey, Felicity, Jodi said I should relieve you so you can go to a meeting Dr. Mason just called," said Matt, startling her, a few minutes later. One of the new nurses who had been hired to take the place of the nurses who were going to the new cardiac center, he moved extremely quietly for being a giant teddy bear of a man at six feet six inches, with the large build to match.

In the last two weeks, Dr. Mason had begun making a habit of calling these last-minute meetings that were making it difficult for her to help fill in while the rest of these new nurses were being trained.

"I'm sorry. I have to leave you." She checked the monitor and saw that Jenny's heart rate had settled into a normal sinus rhythm in the nineties. "But Matt's going to take great care of you. He'll get you admitted and transfer you to the cardiac unit."

"Thank you for taking care of me," Jenny said before shutting her eyes again. The poor woman had been through a lot today. She deserved her rest.

"Believe me, I'd rather be here taking care of you than going to another meeting," Felicity said as she gathered her stethoscope. When she'd accepted the brand-new position of nursing manager at the new clinic, she'd had no idea the number of meetings and the piles of paperwork that were necessary to start the new department.

"Thanks for helping me out. Dr. Mason can be difficult if anyone misses one of his meetings." Felicity couldn't help but feel guilty about leaving her patient with another nurse at this point, but there was nothing that could be done about it. She'd taken the extra shifts in the ER to help out, but everyone knew her first priority had to be her new department.

"No problem," Matt said. "I saw him in the unit introducing some new hire to the ER docs. Rumor says he's some hotshot from London."

A wave of tiny pinpricks rushed over her, making her skin sting and tingle. It was just a coincidence. That was all. New doctors were arriving at Brooklyn Heights every day. Besides, why would Dr. Mason pull everybody in for a meeting concerning some new doctor?

Unless this doctor was a cardiac doctor who had been involved with a specialty ER department. Unless he had been one of the leading members for such a program in his own hospital. The Royal Kensington Hospital in London had such a program. Scott had been there for the planning and opening of that program. Was there a possibility that Scott was actually here?

With the sound of her heart drumming a staccato rhythm in her ear, she tried not to rush through her report to Matt before she hurried off to the meeting room. Her steps became faster as she approached the door. And there, standing once again with his back to her, was the man she had seen earlier in the emergency room. This was getting ridiculous. Was it Scott or not?

Stopping outside the door, she took in everything she could see of him—the perfect cut of a well-tailored suit, one of Scott's indulged weaknesses since graduating from medical school; the broad shoulders, which he'd developed while playing high school football with her brother; and the confident stance, shoulders back and feet solidly planted, which invoked leadership. All these things she could see in this man.

And then he turned, and suddenly her eyes were locked with a pair of hazel ones that mirrored the shock she knew had to be in her own. He was here. Dr. Scott Thomas had returned to New York.

CHAPTER TWO

SCOTT WAS AT a loss for words. Yes, he'd planned on getting up to Hudson to see his parents as soon as possible. And he'd planned, or hoped, to run into Felicity while there, but this? Never had he imagined that he'd find her here in a hospital where he had agreed to work for the next eight weeks.

"Well, this is a surprise," Felicity said as she took a step toward him.

"Scott, this is Felicity Dale, the nurse manager that we've hired to run our new cardiac unit," Dr. Mason said as he walked over to them.

"Scott, why are you here?" Felicity asked him, both of them ignoring the other doctor.

"He's here to help with the opening of the new unit. I told you I was trying to find someone after Dr. Kane had to go on family leave to take care of her mother. There's no telling how long it will take for the poor woman to walk again after her hip fracture. Dr. Kane could be out for months," Dr. Mason continued as the tension between the two of them hummed through the air. Couldn't the man hear it? Feel it?

"I didn't know you were working back in the city," Scott said as he started to recover.

"You know each other?" Dr. Mason asked.

"We worked together in London," Felicity said quickly before Scott had a chance to answer.

He waited for her to add more, but she didn't, which shocked him almost as much as seeing her here. That was it? No mention that the two of them had grown up together? No mention of all the years they had spent as the best of friends?

"Now that I think about it, I do remember something from your résumé about you having experience in London. What a coincidence! This is great! With Dr. Kane having to go on leave, I was so worried about us being ready by the grand opening. But with the two of you working together, I know we'll make it," the older man said as he wrapped one arm around each of their shoulders. "Now, let's get this meeting started."

Dr. Mason moved away from the two of them and headed for the front of the room, giving Scott no choice but to follow him. Hesitating for a moment, he moved closer to Felicity, whispering in her ear, "We'll talk later."

"Sure," she mumbled, before moving away from him and heading for a chair at the large executive table—as far away from him as she could manage.

What was wrong with her? Rather than catching up with an old friend, her tone made it seem like he had suggested that she face a firing squad.

He'd respected her choice to end something that had barely started between the two of them, though he had never understood it, but he'd also given up on understanding why she'd decided to end their friendship too. And now she wanted to pretend that they were barely acquaintances? Was she just still reeling from the shock of this new position they found themselves in?

"I know we're all a little out of sorts with Dr. Kane having to go on leave, but she wanted to tell everyone…"

Scott tried to concentrate on what Dr. Mason was saying. His role in The Kensington Project was to help with the final steps of opening the new cardiac unit in New York City that was being modeled after the London hospital's own center. Part emergency room and part procedural area, it had been highly successful in London and promised to be just as successful here. He'd thought he was ready for the job. Excited, even.

But this? There was no way he could have prepared himself for finding Felicity here in the same hospital as him, let alone having to work on the same project together.

But here he was, sitting at the table with the woman who had once been his best friend, with neither of them even acknowledging that relationship. Were they supposed to go on like this the whole time he was here? She had to know that wouldn't work for either of them.

"And with the experience he has assisting with the setup of the Royal Kensington Hospital's hybrid cardiac center, I know he is the perfect person to help us with the opening of ours. And I've just learned that he and our own Felicity Dale, the nurse manager for our new unit, have actually worked together before in London. With the two of them leading the way, I'm sure we are in for a very successful grand opening and, just as important, a new opportunity to serve our community." Dr. Mason seemed to beam with pleasure every time he mentioned the new center. It was no secret that this was one of the last things the older physician wanted to see completed before he retired. It was one of the first things he'd told Scott that morning when they met. "So now I'm going to turn the meeting over to Dr. Thomas."

Scott stood and looked around the room, his

eyes stopping on Felicity. "It's nice to see all of you here and I look forward to us working together."

He made his eyes move on to the next person beside her and then around to the rest of the staff, but they kept coming back to Felicity. "As Dr. Mason has said, the grand opening of the cardiac center here in New York will be an advancement for patient care that will serve a great need in this community. It promises to streamline the care of cardiac patients, as it will drastically lower the time from ER arrival to intervention, increasing the patient's chances of survival while at the same time helping to decompress the general emergency room, allowing other patients to be seen more quickly. We've seen this happen in London and I'm sure you will see the same results here. Does anyone have any questions?"

He answered a few questions, mostly about the cardiac program in London, then turned the meeting back over to Dr. Mason. After a few reminders concerning the next week's agenda, the meeting was closed and Scott worked his way around the room, stopping as he went to acknowledge introductions from staff members with whom he would be working. Finally he made it to the one person he needed to speak to.

"Fliss, do you have a moment?" There'd be no way for her to deny how well the two of them knew each other with him using the nickname he'd known her by most of his life.

"I can't believe you're here. Why didn't you let me know you were coming?" The blush that followed her statement was an acknowledgment that she was the one who had insisted it would be best if they didn't stay in contact. Of course, he'd refused to accept this until it had become apparent that she wasn't going to take his calls.

Where had things gone so wrong between the two of them? Yes, she had lost her brother, but so had he. Somehow, something that should have brought them closer together had sent the two of them off in different directions. And it seemed by her reaction to his return to New York that she wished for it to stay that way.

"I thought you were still working in Hudson." Hadn't that been the reason she'd refused to go back to London with him? She wanted to be closer to her parents, which was understandable under the circumstances. It had hurt, though, to learn that while he'd been thinking they were starting a new phase in their life together, moving from friends to lovers, she had been planning a life in the States without him.

Before she could answer him, a phone began to buzz, and she pulled the hospital-designated phone out of her lab jacket and read the message out loud. "'Cardiac arrest. Male, fifty-five. ETA fifteen minutes.' I've got to get back to the ER."

"We need to get together." He wasn't going to let her run off without agreeing to talk to him later. There was a lot for the two of them to get caught up on and not just with their personal lives. He had to get up to speed with this new program as well and he needed someone to help him. "Dr. Mason said that the group was getting together at a place across the street after work."

"I can't. I'm still working some shifts in the ER, and when I finish my shift tonight, there are some emails regarding the new unit that I need to address." She glanced back down at the phone in her hand, no doubt figuring out how much time she had till the patient would be arriving.

"I'm sure Dr. Mason is expecting you to attend." While he knew this was true, he did feel a bit guilty about pressuring her to come. He couldn't help but see the dark circles under blue eyes that used to sparkle. There was no sparkle there today.

"Bernard's?" she asked, glancing back at her watch.

Did she really find it that uncomfortable to look him in the eye?

"Yeah, that's the place. We'll talk there." And before she could refuse, he turned and walked away. She wasn't the only one having problems dealing with this situation. Having

Felicity here was going to be a complication for which he was in no way prepared, but if they were going to work together, they needed to start off on the right footing. They didn't have any time to waste to get things back on track for this grand opening. It was important for their careers that everything went smoothly. They were both professionals. They wouldn't let any personal issues get in the way of their jobs.

Now, if only he could convince the knot in his stomach to believe that. And if only he could convince himself that he was going to come out of the next eight weeks without his heart more bruised than the last time he had left New York.

Felicity tried not to get caught staring at the man sitting in the seat beside her. The noise from the crowd at the pub made talking almost impossible—something she was glad of right now. She needed to get her mind wrapped around the fact that Scott was here.

Four hours ago she'd been getting on with

her life, working her job in the emergency room and preparing for her new position as manager of the cardiac center. It had been her dream job. Her everything. She'd been so proud of where her career was going. She had a future to look forward to. She'd applied for the job, hoping it would give her life more purpose.

Yet here Scott was, making her question all the decisions she'd made in the last year and a half, because no matter how much she'd like to deny it, she still felt the same heart-pumping attraction she'd felt for most of her life whenever she was around Scott. It had been hard to fight during her teenage years and had only gotten harder to ignore during her college years. As an adult with no love life for the last eighteen months, she was finding it even harder to ignore now.

But it was only physical. That was all. And Scott would only be here for eight weeks. It wasn't like she was suddenly going to throw herself into his arms. She'd spent most of her adult life ignoring that particular desire.

Except for that one crazy night when they'd broken all the rules of friendship and finally slept together.

No. That wasn't true. They'd taken their relationship into dangerous territory weeks before when what had started as some innocent flirting turned into an attraction that neither of them could ignore. Nights out as friends had suddenly turned into dates in romantic restaurants where they'd become even closer.

It was the change teenage Felicity had always dreamed of for their relationship, while it made the adult woman she had become worry about what this new connection between them would mean for their friendship if things went wrong.

And then there had been that night when she'd thrown all her fears away and embraced everything her body had told her they could have together. And it had been even more than she had ever dreamed of.

Memories flashed through her mind of tangled legs and passionate whispers, her body arching against his as they both cried out their release.

A shiver ran over her skin as it responded.

"Cold?" Scott reached over and handed her his jacket. "It is a little chilly in here."

Unable to tell him where her thoughts had taken her, she didn't argue. Taking his jacket, she draped it over her shoulders. The warmth from the wool and Scott's own body heat made her stomach tighten even more.

"How long have you been here?" His warm breath tickled her cheek as he leaned into her side. His hazel eyes seemed to be searching her face for something. But what? Not that it mattered. She'd developed a good poker face in the last few months; a necessity as she'd started to see the concern in her parents' faces each time she went to visit.

"A year in January." She raised her voice over the noise of the crowd instead of leaning closer as Scott seemed to prefer.

"I thought you were going to stay in town?" He had moved even closer. She blamed the heat from his body and his jacket for her damp palms.

She didn't want to tell him that she'd found the slow pace of their hometown upstate New York community hospital unbearable after the excitement of working at a London hospital—something that he'd told her would happen.

"They made me an offer I couldn't refuse," she said, quoting from what she knew was one of Scott's favorite movies. She watched his lips lift into the half smile that had never failed to charm her. Her own smile couldn't be hidden.

"Okay, so you were right. The pace of a small hospital was too slow for me. Not that the people weren't nice—they were. I just didn't fit in there." She didn't have to tell him that her work life was all she'd had then. All she still had.

But it's important work. My patients need me and that's what matters. It's enough.

Then why did it seem she was having to remind herself of that now? The last eighteen months had been hard. The loss of her brother had been hard on all of them, but she'd made it through by concentrating on her parents and her work. And now she had her dream job and it was all the future she needed right now, no matter how much that stupid voice in her head kept telling her she needed more.

Their waitress began passing out their group's orders and Scott leaned back into his seat. She took a deep breath and would have relaxed except she caught the scent of spicy deep woods and salty sea breezes.

He still wore the cologne she had given him all those Christmases ago.

He'd been a senior in high school that year, and the crush she'd had on him had been growing for those last two years. She'd saved her babysitting money all that fall and gone alone to the department store where she spent over an hour looking for the perfect gift for Scott.

The memory of how her brother, Leo, had made fun of the gift was bittersweet now. But wasn't everything bittersweet when it came to her and Scott? There was so much of the two of them entangled with her memories of Leo that she found it impossible to think about one without thinking about the other. They'd both been the most important people in her life except for her parents. And now she had neither one of them.

"You're not eating," Scott said as once more he leaned closer to her.

She cut a piece of the medium-rare steak she had ordered and studied it. Her stomach churned at the thought of eating it. She couldn't do it.

Suddenly it was too much. All of it. The surprise of seeing Scott. Knowing they would be working together again. The memories of Leo with the two of them. It was just too much.

"I need to go. I'm sorry. I forgot about an email that must be sent out tonight," she said to the group along with Scott as she handed him back his jacket. If she sat there one more minute, she would lose it, and she wasn't going to embarrass herself in front of her colleagues like that. Opening her purse, she put several bills on the table, then stood up. Without another word she headed for the door that would lead her out to the street where she could lose herself in the crowd. Not that she thought Scott would follow her. He wouldn't. He was too much of a professional to rush off and leave the rest of the group, even if he wanted to.

Besides, why would he after the way everything between the two of them had ended? Scott had undoubtedly moved on with his life by now. If only she had the strength to do the same thing. Because eventually she would have to face Scott, and it would be a lot easier for both of them if she could put all the old feelings she'd always had for him behind her so that maybe at the very least the two of them would be able to work together again without letting their past get in the way.

CHAPTER THREE

SCOTT WATCHED AS Felicity rushed out the door. Had he said something to upset her? He'd tried to keep things light and friendly without bringing up any subjects that could cause issues between them, yet still things had gone wrong. Could it have gone any worse?

Of course it could. All it would take was one conversation with Dr. Mason and she could have him sent back to London. Not that he thought she would do that. While he couldn't seem to recognize this woman Felicity had become now, he knew inside that she was still the same fair person she had always been. They just needed to find some safe ground where they could communicate.

He'd spent hours imagining what it would

be like to see Felicity again, but nothing had prepared him for this.

He'd imagined seeing her on the street of their hometown. She'd turn and see him, her eyes lighting up with joy, and then she'd walk into his arms.

He'd imagined casually dropping by her parents' home and finding her there. Once again she'd be happy to see him and once again she'd walk into his arms as if the last few months had never taken place.

Ever since he'd been told he would be returning to the States, he'd thought of scenario after scenario and, yes, unrealistically each scenario had ended with her in his arms. Not once had he imagined that she would instead be running out of a restaurant to get away from him.

He wanted to blame it on the fact that neither of them had been prepared for seeing each other this way. Just like they hadn't been prepared the morning they got the phone call telling them that Leo was dead. If they'd had a few more days, a week or a month before that call, maybe things would have turned out differently.

But they hadn't been given that time. And now they were both back in New York and once more they didn't have a lot of time. But he couldn't make this about him and Felicity. This was about the job and getting it done right and on time.

There wasn't time for him to spend wondering about what might have been. From the way Felicity had acted when she had seen him, that would be a waste of both their time. She would come around to the idea of working with him again. She was too much of a professional not to. And they'd always made a good team, so there was nothing to worry about there. All they needed to do was concentrate on the task ahead of them and leave their personal problems out of it. But first maybe they needed to clear the air.

He stood and excused himself.

"Fliss, wait!" he called as he caught up with her a moment before she made it out the door. For a minute he thought she hadn't heard him.

Or was it that she was pretending not to hear him? "Hold up."

She stopped and turned toward him. His gaze was again drawn to the dark circles around those blue eyes that had once stared up at him with pleasure. Where was the sparkle? The laughter? The welcoming smile that was as much a part of her as her own name? There was no welcoming smile for him now.

He couldn't help but feel anger toward his lost friend. Had Leo even thought about what he was doing to the lives of the people who loved him when he'd taken his own? Scott knew that wasn't fair to his friend; Leo had been in a dark place inside his own mind, but at times Scott couldn't help but feel anger toward Leo for leaving them this way.

"We need to talk," he said, moving out of the way so another diner could exit the restaurant. When she didn't argue, he looked around the lobby for a more appropriate setting for this conversation. Finding a small corner away from the door, he walked toward it. For a moment she gazed out the door, and he thought she wouldn't follow him. She seemed to gather herself, her back becoming straighter and her chin coming up. This was more the woman he knew.

"I'm sorry if I was a bit abrupt. It's been a long day and I really think it would be better if we talked later. This has all been a bit of a shock," she said.

He recognized that stubborn look in her eyes. He'd seen it many times over the years. There would be no getting her to change her mind right now.

"I'm in meetings all day tomorrow. What about dinner after work?" He wasn't going to let her go without pinning her down on a time. He'd known things wouldn't be straightforward between the two of them when they did meet again, but he hadn't expected this. Of course, he hadn't expected the changes he saw in Fliss either.

She gave a short laugh and shook her head. "I barely have time to sleep right now. I still have shifts to work in the emergency room until I go full-time on the new unit. Plus,

I'm working almost full-time hours trying to keep everything going so that we can make our grand opening on time."

"All work and no play…" He left it open to finish. It was a stupid game of quotes and proverbs they'd played when they were in school and continued through the years.

"…makes Felicity a successful leader in her new manager role," she said as she rolled her eyes at him, a sign that the old cocky Fliss was inside this woman somewhere. He just needed to be patient, though that was the last thing he was feeling right now. There was so much he wanted to say, but she was right. Meeting like this had been a shock to both of them. They'd both be more prepared to deal with this after a good night's sleep.

"Okay, I'll see how my schedule goes tomorrow. Maybe we can get together before you leave for the day." He'd make it happen one way or the other. Whether she thought so or not, there were things that needed to be dealt with between the two of them if they were going to be able to work together again.

"Sure, tomorrow sounds great, but I think you need to get back to your dinner now. Dr. Mason isn't the most patient of men. Good night," she said as she hitched her purse up on her shoulder and headed away.

He waited until he saw her disappear into the sidewalk crowd before he made his way back to his table.

"Is everything okay?" Dr. Mason asked from across the table. The older man was not a fool. He had to have noticed Felicity's reaction to Scott.

"Everything's going to be fine," he answered with confidence, trying to convince himself as much as his new colleague. Something told him this would be the most difficult assignment he had ever been given.

Because this job and the chance he had of any type of future relationship with Felicity depended on it.

"There you are," Scott said from beside her. "I thought I'd missed you."

Felicity looked up from the computer where

she'd been finishing the charting on her last patient for the day. It had been so long since she'd seen him dressed in his white lab jacket. He was every bit as handsome as she re-membered. She tried to ignore the shiver of recognition that ran through her. This was something she was going to have to get used to now and she didn't dare let Scott see how his presence affected her.

"I was just about to leave. It's been a long day," she said as she started shutting down the computer. The holiday season was close, and with tourist numbers in the city growing, the number of people seen in the ER would increase till after the first of the year.

"Maybe I can walk you out?" Scott asked as she stood.

"That's fine." She had planned to catch a taxi outside the emergency-room entrance, so at least it would be a short talk.

A cold wind blew through the ambulance bay as the doors shut behind her. She wrapped her arms around herself as they stopped for a crew of EMTs to roll a stretcher loaded with a man who looked as miserable as she felt right then. Tired and cold were not a good combination.

"I'm going this way," she said, pointing toward the line of taxis as he started in the direction of the car park.

"I can give you a ride. It will give us more time to talk," Scott said as his hand came up behind her to rest on her back. She started to move away from him when suddenly she was pulled into his arms.

The weight of his arms around her as he clasped her tight to his body brought back memories that made her head swim, but the screech of tires and a woman's screams for help brought her right back to reality.

"I need help!" the woman cried as she threw open her driver's door, then moved to the back door of the car. "My son, he's not breathing."

As Felicity grabbed a stretcher that had been left by the door, Scott rushed to the woman's side.

"What happened?" Scott asked as he pulled

the young boy out of the car and laid him down on the stretcher.

The boy's color was a dusky blue and Fliss checked for a pulse before starting compressions. There was no sign of trauma that she could see and teenage boys did not just go into cardiac arrest.

"It's my fault," the woman cried as Scott pushed the stretcher into the entrance and began calling for help. "It's my medicine. He took all my medicine."

"I've got this," one of the EMTs Felicity had seen earlier said as he took over the compressions. Other staff members joined them as they rushed the boy into the first empty room.

"Felicity, find out what it was he took," Scott called out to her as he told another nurse to draw up some Narcan.

"Got it," she called back as she put her arm around the shaking woman and led her aside. "We need your help. Can you tell me what happened? What did your son take?"

"It was my pain meds my doctor prescribed me when I hurt my back. I think it's called

Norco. I've only taken it once and I keep it put away. I guess he found it in my dresser when I was at work. Is he okay? Is he going to be okay?" the woman pleaded. "He's been so depressed since that girl broke up with him, but I didn't think he'd do this. Not my Butchy. He's too smart for this."

A cold chill ran up Felicity's spine as she realized this hadn't been just another kid suffering from an accidental overdose while experimenting with their parents' medication.

"Is he going to be okay?" the boy's mother asked again. "Please tell me he's going to be okay."

"We've got his heartbeat back," Scott said as he joined them. "The emergency-room doctor is in with him now, but he'll give you an update as soon as he can. Come this way and I'll show you where you can wait."

The trip to Felicity's apartment was quiet with neither of them talking after she gave Scott her address.

"I checked with Dr. Adams before he left.

The boy's going to be okay," Scott said as he parked the car in front of her apartment.

"I know. I checked with his nurse. He's already fighting against the ventilator." She'd made sure the boy's mother would be let in as soon as possible too. She knew what it was like to sit in that room and wait for news of whether your loved one was going to survive or not. "His mom said this was over a girl. A girl. He wanted to give up living because of some teenage girl. What sense does that make?"

"It's not ever going to make sense to us," Scott said. She knew they were no longer talking about the boy they'd left in the ER.

"If we understood, would it make it better?" she asked. "It's all those questions of why and what you could have done to stop it that eat at you. They never stop."

"But there comes a time you have to let it go," Scott said. "You know that."

She did know that. She just didn't know how it was possible. Letting go of the guilt and pain would be like letting go of her brother. Let go of the big brother who had always been there for her? It would be like giving up a piece of her heart. She wouldn't be able to live without it.

"If life were just that easy," she said before unbuckling her seat belt and opening the car door.

"Look," she said as she turned back to him, "you don't have to worry about the job. I've got my part in opening the new unit under control. And as far as working together, maybe putting our past behind us is what we need to do."

"Can you do that?" Scott asked. His eyes held hers and she fought against looking away. Somehow she had to convince him that she could work with him without it affecting the job they'd been given.

"Sometimes, you just have to let it go." Turning, she rushed out of the car and ran into her building, shutting the door behind her before the first tear fell.

"We're going to take care of you. You did the right thing calling 911 when the pain started,"

Felicity assured the man clutching his left arm as she applied the pads of the cardiac monitor. She'd bet her bachelor's degree that the man was having an ST-elevation myocardial infarction, which meant time was not on their side. The sooner the interventional cardiologist could confirm her suspicions, the sooner they could get this patient to the heart cath lab.

She looked at her watch and wrote the time the patient had arrived down on her paperwork. One of the first things Scott had taught her in the cardiac department in London was how important door-to-balloon time was in achieving the best outcome for the patient. It had been just a little over thirty minutes since the man's chest pain had started.

This was why it was so vital to get the new cardiac center open. With its emergency triage abilities and its new procedural area, they could streamline the process, which meant cutting the time a cardiac patient spent in the regular emergency room. From the web meetings she had attended in the last week, she knew Scott was spearheading the procedures to identify these patients when they arrived in the emergency room.

"It's a STEMI," she said to the ER doctor who had come to stand by her as they both studied the monitors.

"Okay, let's start the chest pain protocol and get an EKG to confirm. I'll go call the doctor who's on," he said as he walked away.

"Where's the doctor going?" the man asked, his voice cracking with pain and fear. "Can I see my wife?"

She started applying the EKG pads so that the strip would be available when the doctor returned.

"You need a specialist, so he's going to go call the cardiologist who'll be here in just a few minutes to check everything out. As soon as I can, I'll get your wife in to see you. Try to be still for just a few seconds."

She waited for a second, then hit the button, and the strip started printing. Studying the rhythm displayed on the paper, she knew she had been right. It was a classic MI. She sent the electronic record to the patient's chart so that the two doctors could review it, then looked at the clock over the stretcher. It had only been fifteen minutes since the patient had rolled into the room, but it seemed so much longer.

"I'll be back with something to help with the pain, and the cardiologist will be right in." The fact that she had to leave the room to get the medication while what he really needed was her at his bedside was another reason that the new cardiac center was so important. She'd met some resistance from the pharmacy about having a medicine dispenser in each of the new state-of-the-art exam rooms, and the department's budget had taken a big hit, but she'd won that fight.

Returning to the room, she found the heart cath team already preparing to transport her patient.

"That was fast," she said to Sandy, one of the nurses who soon would be part of her own staff.

"Dr. Thomas reviewed the chart and agreed

that it was a STEMI. He's waiting to talk to the patient. Can you bring his wife over for us?" the other nurse said as she switched the patient to a portable monitor.

"I'm going to get her right now," Felicity told her patient as she arranged the blankets more securely around him. "Dr. Thomas is one of the top cardiologists I know. He'll explain everything to you. You're in the best of hands."

She watched for a second as the patient was rolled out of the room. Then she headed to the waiting room to find her patient's wife. The fact that Scott was picking up some of the shifts in the intervention cath lab, which had been left empty when Dr. Kane had taken leave, was not a surprise. While he seemed to be comfortable with the administrative details he would have to handle with this project, she knew his heart would always be in patient care, and she had no doubt that Dr. Mason had considered his procedural experience and reputation when hiring him.

Somehow she had been able to avoid Scott

for the last four days, but now with the new center on track to open soon, it was the last day she would be working in the emergency room. Instead of attending meetings remotely and working on the new unit following her shifts in the ER, from now on all her time would be spent getting ready for their grand opening. Of course, part of her was just like Scott; she preferred the hands-on patient care, which wouldn't start till after the opening.

Preparing herself for both an upset wife and a doctor whose mere presence set loose a bucket of butterflies in her stomach, she headed out into the waiting room. She wouldn't be able to avoid seeing Scott any longer.

Scott left the cath lab feeling good about his patient's outcome. It helped that Felicity and the ER doctor had diagnosed the patient quickly and that the rest of the heart team had responded, making the patient's door-to-balloon time below the ninety-minute threshold that was the standard. The group he had been sent to work with here in New York were all professionals, which was making his job a lot easier. But he couldn't help but notice the way Felicity had fled the room as soon as he finished talking to her patient's wife. He knew she was busy in the always-crowded emergency room, and bless her for helping out with their staffing crunch, but that wasn't the problem. She was still avoiding him, and it had to be dealt with if the two of them were going to work together.

He'd tried to clear the air between them, but she remained distant. He'd given her space to accept the fact that he was here in her hospital, and now it was time for them to move on. There were a lot of details they needed to go over on the nursing side of the new center. As the nursing manager, it was her job to work with him, and that was impossible for them to do if she kept avoiding being in the same room with him. Enough was enough.

Placing a call to the emergency room, he requested that Fliss come to the office—*her* office—that Dr. Mason had him using in the new department. He had no doubt that seeing him sitting behind what was supposed to be her desk was something that would set her off. She'd always been the first one to call him out on acting privileged just because he had a medical degree hanging on his wall. He couldn't wait to see her reaction to the fact that he had moved in and made himself at home, since the only time she seemed to use the office was after he had left for the day. The office was big enough for the two of them to share, though that didn't seem to be something that she would do. Thirty minutes later—and, yes, he was sure that Fliss had kept him waiting on purpose—there was a knock at his door.

"You wanted to see me?" she asked as she stepped through the doorway.

Seeing her standing in front of him wearing those bright blue scrubs that had always been her favorite, he was struck by the truth of those words. Yes, he'd wanted to see her. He'd wanted to see her every day since he'd left New York. He'd spent every day of the last eighteen months missing seeing those blue eyes that seemed to sparkle with humor and those just-a-little-bit-too-wide lips that had seemed to smile with joy whenever the two of them had been together.

But those eyes showed none of that humor today. Instead they had a wariness that he had never seen before. And there certainly was no joy in her smile. He watched, fascinated, as her teeth came out and bit down on her bottom lip. Was she nervous about seeing him? Then her face lost all signs of emotion, as if she had suddenly taken control and she had to hide whatever it was she was feeling from him.

But he knew that it had to be killing her to hold that blank mask in place. Fliss had never been one for holding back her feelings or opinions. It was one of the things he had always admired about her. If she was pissed off at you, you knew it. There was no game you had to play to find out what had upset her. The fact that she was holding everything in now was not a good sign. He wanted his old Fliss back, the one who would be chewing him out right now for his high-handed demand that she come see him.

But she wasn't his anymore and he needed to remember that. He needed to treat her just like another member of the team.

"Please, take a seat." This time he saw a spark of anger as she narrowed her eyes at him. Then it was gone and the new all-business version of Felicity returned. "I thought this might be a good time for the two of us to talk. I've been able to speak with everyone involved with the grand opening of the new unit, except for you. For some reason you've turned down every invitation I've emailed you, and every time I try to talk to you, you deny there's a problem or you run away. We used to talk about everything." She'd given him no option but to bring up their past. Hopefully it wouldn't make things between them worse. "I understand that my presence here was a surprise, but it's time for us to move past that. I need to know if you're going to be able to work with me on this."

She blinked rapidly with a deer-in-the-headlights look that told him nothing of what was going on behind her bright blue eyes. What was it going to take to get past this wall she had built around her emotions? And more important, why did she feel she needed that wall between the two of them? Finally she took the chair in front of the desk.

"I apologize," she said, her eyes now meeting his and holding. "I have been busy trying to help with the emergency-room staffing, but today was my last shift. I'll be able to put all my time into preparing for the center's opening now. And, yes, I understand that we will need to work closer together from this point on."

She hadn't given him much, but it was a start. Still, it would be better if they came to a clear understanding.

"I'm not saying that you haven't been doing your job, Fliss." He saw the small jerk of her body when he used her nickname. It seemed she didn't want any reminder of the relationship that the two of them had shared in the past. If she didn't like him calling her by the name her family and friends used, he would have to respect that. If it helped for the two of them to work together, he'd avoid it from now on. "I've seen the emails. You've done a remarkable job organizing the department. But I'm sure you're aware that with just five weeks left till we open the new unit, there will be more hands-on work needed from both of us. I need to know that it isn't going to be a problem. I need to know that the two of us can work together."

"There won't be a problem," Felicity said, her chin coming up with a look of determination that he had seen many times. "I plan to do everything possible to make this grand opening perfect. This is *my* hospital. I'm invested in its success."

Staring into those deep blue eyes, he knew that she was telling him the truth. She'd do whatever she had to in order to make her department the best. Even if it meant working with him.

But he wanted more than that. He wanted

the way it used to be when they worked together. He wanted the two of them to be a real team. Together they could make this project the best one he had ever been involved with. He could go back to London knowing he had made a difference when his time here was over, and that was important to him.

No, he had accepted that they could never go back to the way things were before Leo's death, but was it too much to ask for the two of them to at least get along while he was here?

"Okay, then. How about we do a walk-through of the unit together? I'd like to see the nurses' side of the patient-flow process," Scott said before standing. It was time to see if this unspoken truce between the two of them would hold up.

Felicity wasn't sure how she found herself with Scott in the deserted new unit when she'd spent the last four days doing everything she could to avoid him. But she had known that eventually she would have to face the fact that they would be working together.

While most of the remodeling work had been completed earlier in the month, late equipment arrivals and some changes that had been required after the approval of the medicine-dispensing machines meant there was still some construction work being done. Unfortunately the crews that had been working had already gone for the day.

"I like the fact that you've provided for supplies to be kept in each individual room, but what about the restocking?" Scott asked as he opened one of the built-in glass-doored cabinets.

"Each nurse will be assigned a set of room numbers each shift. It will be their responsibility to restock their rooms when they turn it over before the next patient arrives," Felicity said as she moved around the room, trying to concentrate on the work that had been finished as well as what still needed to be done before the rest of the equipment was installed.

But like the night at the restaurant, the sight

of Scott brought back too many memories. No wonder Scott was afraid she wouldn't be able to work with him. Every time they were together, she became overwhelmed with emotions that she hadn't felt for months.

After Leo's death, she had felt nothing. She'd been numbed by the shock of his suicide and the loss of the big brother to whom she'd always been so close. It was all she could do to put up a good front for her parents so that she could support them. Then the numbness had been gone and all the pain had rushed inside of her. Not only the pain of losing Leo, but the pain of having to send Scott back to London without her. She'd had to accept that there could never be a future for the two of them with his life in London and her place in New York with her parents. She'd made the right decision sending him back to a job to which he had dedicated his career, but she'd had to work hard to find a way to deal with the pain and still function. After six months of barely surviving while also helping her parents cope with their own pain, she'd been able to make a life here at work, which gave her a sense of belonging and purpose and took her focus off the pain of her brother's loss that would always be there.

Now Scott was here disturbing the peace she had found. Because every time she saw him, all she could think about was their time together in London when they had finally both been in the right place at the right time. They'd taken the chance on having more than just the friendship they'd shared since childhood.

She'd spent her whole adult life waiting to have Scott see her as a woman instead of as his best friend's little sister or as a best friend in her own right. And even though she'd first been concerned about what it could mean for their friendship, it had been worth it. It had been intense and magical and everything she had known in her heart it would be. And then it had to come to an end with one phone call.

Now she didn't even know how to carry on a conversation with the man whom she had once dreamed of spending her whole life with. But for the next two months she needed to find a way to make this work, because she'd made the hardest sacrifice she could imagine by sending Scott away, and she didn't know if she would be strong enough to watch him leave again.

No, she could and would do this. She set her mind back to the job at hand. She would make this work. This unit was the most important thing she had in her life right now. She just had to find a way of dealing with Scott as she would any other coworker. She'd managed to hide her feelings for him all through high school when he'd spent most of his time at her house, hanging out with her brother. She'd spent hour upon hour trying to listen through the thin wall between her and her brother's rooms, waiting to hear Scott say something, anything, about what he thought of her. Until finally she'd realized that he had no deep thoughts about or longing for her as she had for him. Still, she'd been happy with the friendship that had grown between them as she had gotten older.

All she needed now was to do the same thing for the few hours that she was at work. She was older and wiser. His place was in London and her place was here, where she could watch over her parents. Nothing had changed in the last eighteen months. It was time to grow up. She was an adult and she needed to act like it. She had responsibilities to her parents now that Leo was gone.

She embraced her pep talk and turned her attention back to her job and the exam rooms they were discussing.

"I like the color," Scott mentioned as he motioned toward a wall where monitors were being installed.

The painters had begun covering the walls with the pale gray paint that would match the furniture, which had been ordered months earlier but still hadn't arrived. She made a note on her computer pad to give the warehouse a call the next day. "We didn't want to go with the same white of the emergency room. We felt this would be more calming."

"And the new monitors are going to be amazing. I've sent the manufacturer information back to our purchasing agent in London so that when it's time to upgrade our unit, we can get a price on them," Scott said as he moved out the glass door and into the hallway that would take them back to the office. "And having the medication dispensers in each room will be amazing. I still don't know how that was managed. That many machines, even though they're smaller, must have been expensive."

"It was the first thing I lobbied for when I got the position. I felt like it was something that had to be there so that the nurse could not only give the medications quickly, but also remain in the room with the patient as much as possible." She couldn't help but feel a bit of pride that she had impressed him.

"I'd love to review the list of medications that will be stocked," he said as they made their way back to the office.

"I had all the medications that would be kept on the unit approved by Dr. Kane before she left," Felicity said.

"And she consulted with all the cardiologists that will be working on the unit, I'm sure, but we both know things get forgotten or overlooked. It wouldn't hurt to give the doctors another look so that when we do open, there won't be any complaints."

He had a valid point and Dr. Kane hadn't informed her which doctors had been allowed to see the medication list that had been put together from their own past experiences. There could have been someone left out, and doctors did not like being left out of decisions that impacted their patients' care.

"I can email you the list before I leave today," she said.

"It's looking good, but I think we can agree that there is still a lot to do before opening next month," Scott said as they stopped outside the office door.

She looked down at the list she had compiled in the last hour. There was a lot to do, but it was very doable. "True, but we're still on schedule."

"But it's a tight schedule. One thing goes wrong and we'll be playing catch-up for the rest of the month," Scott said as he opened the door. "Now, how do you want to share the office now that the two of us will be working the same hours?"

Share the office? That would never work. "I really don't need the office right now. It's mostly here for me to have any private conversations I might need with the staff or the physicians. Most of the time I'll be working with them in the unit."

She'd be happy to work in the nurses' lounge as long as it put some distance between the two of them.

Sitting down behind the desk, he leaned back in the office chair and studied her. It seemed they had come full circle and ended right back where this conversation had started.

"We're going to be working together closely, and I'll be honest—I don't understand why it should be that difficult. To be exact, it should be simpler. We've worked together before without any problems. But this time things are different. *We're* different. You've agreed that we have to put the past behind us, but I don't understand it, or what happened, and I'm worried that it's going to affect this project," Scott said, his eyes never leaving her.

She remembered the pep talk she had given herself earlier. She couldn't keep letting old emotions and memories cloud the here and now.

"If we concentrate on the job, I know we can make this work," she assured him.

"So, we go at this with a fresh start. A new beginning?" he asked.

"Yes," she agreed, "a new beginning."

He continued to study her for a minute before he nodded his head. "Okay, let's get together tomorrow after lunch and go over the rest of the construction details. The last thing we want is for something to come up that will cause a postponement of the opening."

Felicity nodded her head in agreement and

then headed back into the ER to finish her shift. It was going to take more than a pep talk to prepare her for the next few weeks, but the thought of a new beginning with Scott did show some promise, even if working close to him would not be easy. Because no matter how much she talked bravely of putting their past behind them, she knew there would always be a part of her buried in that past.

CHAPTER FOUR

FELICITY COULDN'T BELIEVE how much work was involved in starting up the new unit. She'd spent every day for the last two weeks juggling staffing schedules, attending meetings and having very heated discussions with the purchasing department that was still negotiating with the delivery of the unit's furniture. And that didn't take into consideration all the last-minute details and decisions the construction crew had started coming to her to solve.

And then there was Scott. He was everywhere she turned. She wasn't sure when the man had become so needy. He was always needing questions answered, always needing progress reports. And now there was the multitude of doctors that he had brought to her because he needed her to orient them on the new process of triaging chest pain patients in their new location. It seemed that it would never end.

But along with his apparent neediness had come her ability to deal with him better on a professional basis. She was so used to seeing him now that his presence was no longer causing the heart-thumping reaction that it had two weeks ago.

Okay, maybe there were still a few palpitations when he sat a little too close to her like he was right now in the crowded meeting room, but all in all she thought she was handling things a lot better than she had hoped. All she had to do was make it through this last meeting of the day and she'd be off for the long Thanksgiving holiday.

"My mother called this morning," Scott said as he moved closer and whispered.

"That's nice," she said through gritted teeth as those irritating palpitations returned. Why did the man feel so welcome to invade her personal space? Oh, yeah, because he had all but lived there before.

"She spoke with your mother last night." He seemed to be waiting for her to respond, though she wasn't sure why. She was very aware that their mothers spoke daily. The two of them had been close since their own childhood.

"My mom was keen to assure your mother that I would be very happy to give you a ride home tomorrow," he said.

She choked on nothing but air as she took in his words. Covering her mouth, she cleared her throat and took a sip of water as the staff members in front of her turned around, embarrassing her even more.

She cleared her throat again until she could find her voice. "You don't need to take me. I've already bought a Metro ticket."

"What and have our mothers mad at me the whole time I'm home?" he whispered back to her, giving her no doubt that it hadn't been his idea. He probably had no more of a desire to spend his morning stuck in a car with her than she did with him. But that didn't change the fact that their mothers would not understand why they couldn't share the ride.

Finally the meeting came to an end, giving her a chance to escape.

"Whoa," Scott called out as he grabbed her hand. "We need to talk about this. You can't leave me taking the heat when I show up without you."

"There isn't anything to talk about. I've made arrangements. I don't need a ride to my parents' house." Her voice sounded whiny and childish even to her own ears as she pulled her hand from his while trying to ignore the buzz of attraction that had always run through her when Scott touched her.

"That's fine. I just need you to call my mother and explain that to her," he said as he moved back to his seat and retrieved his computer.

All signs of attraction disappeared. "I can't do that. You know how she and my mother are. They never take no for an answer."

One dark brown eyebrow lifted as he stared at her.

"Can't you just tell her that you didn't see me?" Not that his mother would take that as an excuse.

"You want me to lie to my mother?" he asked.

"What? Like you've never lied to your mother before? What about the time you and Leo sneaked out to meet Allison and Sarah out by the lake?" She realized her mistake as soon as the words were out.

"How do you know about that?" Scott asked as they joined the group exiting the room.

"I guess Leo told me." There was no way she was admitting that she had been listening through the door that night. Maybe there had been a time she would have been okay confessing her less-than-honest deeds, but not now. Besides, they weren't supposed to be bringing up their past. Of course, it had been her who brought it up first.

That darned eyebrow rose again.

"Okay, just tell her that I had already made plans," she said. And what explanation would she come up with for her own mother, who would see this as an act of extreme rudeness? Being stubborn wasn't a good reason for upsetting her mother. Her mother had hounded her for months for details of what had happened between her and Scott after he'd returned to London and they lost contact. Both their mothers were undoubtedly thrilled they were working together again.

There was no way she was going to win this one. The trip would be uncomfortable, that was for sure, but it would make her mother happy to see the two of them together, and that was what really mattered.

"There's no getting out of this, is there?" she asked as they moved down the hall together.

"I'll pick you up at eight," he said as he looked down at his watch. "See you then."

She watched him as he hurried out of the building toward the doctors' parking lot, unable to keep from wondering where he was off to in such a hurry. Did the popular Dr. Thomas have a date? And where had that thought even come from?

She was supposed to be concentrating on their work, not their past, and it was proving to be much harder than she had thought. She felt like she was back in middle school, where the green monster of jealousy had consumed her every time she'd seen Scott out with one of his high school dates. But that was the past. She was a grown woman now and he was a grown man. That thought didn't make her feel any better. They had definitely been two grown-ups sharing very grown-up actions when they had spent the night together.

And that was definitely not something she wanted to think about right now. Groaning, she pulled her coat on, then shoved her knitted cap on her head. The weather station had called for the temperatures to dip into the twenties. She'd have to pack some extra layers, as it would be even colder in their small hometown of Hudson.

Suddenly she stopped in the middle of the sidewalk. People passed on each side of her while she thought of what had just happened.

No matter how uncomfortable her thoughts

were now, she and Scott had actually had a conversation. Not the conversations they had been having for the last couple of weeks that had been centered round their work. They'd had a personal discussion that had included their lives outside of work—at least, as it pertained to their parents—and it hadn't been awful. Was it possible that by starting anew, they could someday return to being friends? Could she accept friendship after losing the chance of having so much more? She'd accepted that friendship was all they could have years ago and had found a way to make it work. Was it possible for her to do it again?

Starting back down the sidewalk, she suddenly felt lighter than she had in weeks. Maybe there was some hope for the two of them to find a way to have some type of relationship once his time here was over. But at what cost? Could she let herself get close to him again without wanting more? Could she lower those fragile walls she had put up to protect herself from being hurt again and take a chance on a friendship that had meant so much to her? It wasn't like she was looking for more than friendship. Nothing had changed since he had gone back to London. Whether her parents wanted to admit it or not, they needed her close by.

It was going to be a long drive back to their hometown. All she could do was wait and see what spending more time alone together would bring. Hopefully, at least for their parents' sake, they would be able to make this work.

The strain of trying to keep up a conversation with Scott without touching on any subjects that would bring up a past that they had agreed not to discuss had Felicity closing her eyes and pretending to sleep while they traveled north in the high-end sedan that Scott had rented for the time he was in New York.

The first hour had gone by quickly as they'd discussed some of the projects to which they'd agreed to give priority status once they were back at work on Monday. Then Scott informed her that their parents had planned a dinner together tonight at his parents' house and it had been decided that Christmas dinner would be at her parents' house this year. After that, the conversation had sagged and she hadn't wanted to risk the comfortable mood between the two of them by bringing up the fact that it would be the first year they'd have Christmas at their house without Leo.

So now she sat, eyes closed, her head resting against the back of the seat while her mind brought up memory after memory of Christmas in her childhood home with her parents and Leo. Christmas without Leo was impossible to imagine. Last year they'd all still been suffering from an all-consuming grief and the holidays had been easy to ignore. But this year they would have to face it. Her parents would take it hard, but she would be there for them. They wouldn't go through it alone.

"I know you're not sleeping," Scott said from beside her.

He was wearing the cologne she loved, and

she breathed it in as she tried to make her body relax into the seat.

"My parents know this year will be hard for you and your parents. They'll be there to help. We all will."

She heard the concern in his voice and wanted to crawl deeper into the seat. She wasn't stupid. She knew her parents were as concerned about her as she was about them, and she had no doubt that her mother had expressed those concerns to Scott's mother. She was once again glad that their parents had never known the change that had taken place in her and Scott's relationship before they'd learned of Leo's death. Having both of their mothers involved in their love life would have made it even harder to send Scott away. Neither one of them would have understood how helpless she had felt thousands of miles away from her parents when they needed her the most. Nor would they have understood the guilt she felt about being so far away from her brother when he too had needed her. She'd let her brother down. She would not make that mistake again. The only other option would have been for Scott to move back to the States and she wasn't going to let that happen. They'd all been so proud of him when he'd been offered the job at the Royal Kensington Hospital. Giving that up for her would have been wrong.

She'd been so confused about what had happened to her brother that she'd been in no condition to make any type of commitment to a relationship, even if it was to Scott. It had seemed that everything she believed in was shattered. How could the brother who had always been so happy on the outside been so depressed on the inside that he took his own life? And why hadn't she noticed it during their weekly phone calls? She hadn't noticed it because she had been too tied up in her own life instead of looking out for her family.

And if she had been so wrong about her brother, what was to say she wasn't wrong about how she felt about Scott? What if she was just one more relationship to Scott? There had been no mention of a commitment. She'd watched him with girls, then later women, and had always wanted to know what it would feel like to be the one who won Scott's heart. But she had no reason to think he wouldn't have moved on from her just like he had dozens of times before with others. No, it was best that things had ended the way they had without their parents being involved.

"Your parents have been great. A lot of people I thought were my parents' friends came around at first, but then they kind of disappeared. I think the grief they were going through was just too much for others to deal with," she said, trying to return the focus to her parents.

"And you? Did you have someone to support you?" he asked.

Just what was he asking? Did he want to know if there was someone else in her life? He had to know that hadn't been true—at least, not when Leo died. She'd been in London and spent all her time with him. There was no way he could think that she had broken things off because of another man.

"I would have been there if you'd let me," he murmured softly.

"I thought we agreed not to talk about the past." He had no right to bring this all up again.

She'd known he loved his job in London, and even though he might not have understood it then, time had to have shown him that they'd made the right decision to break things off between them. Besides, it was water under the bridge now. There was nothing good for either of them that could come out of reliving that decision.

"I know you're aware that caregivers are the last ones to ask for help when they need it," he said.

She felt a tiny stab in her heart. He hadn't been asking about her as his once-upon-a-time lover. He was just showing concern for a coworker and old friend.

"I have my parents," she said as she turned her head to stare out the window, looking for something to change the subject. "Look, there's a Christmas tree farm."

She squealed as he hit the brakes, then quickly turned the car into the small parking lot that was already crowded with families looking for that one perfect tree. "What are you doing?"

"Isn't that pretty obvious?" Scott asked as he opened his car door, letting a gust of wind into the car. "Better grab your hat and gloves—the temperature's turning icy. Dad called this morning to say they had a lot of snow overnight."

Grabbing her coat from the back seat, she pulled out gloves and her hat, then opened her door. Her eyes immediately went to the small stand that was selling hot chocolate. She turned around and pulled her purse from the car, then shut the door.

She got a glimpse of Scott over at a stand selling Christmas wreaths as she stood in line for the warm chocolate magic that she hoped would heat both her hands and her stomach. After paying for the drinks, she began her search for Scott again.

Avoiding the children who ran in and out

of the trees that had already been chopped down, she started down the middle aisle, finally spotting Scott in the last row, where a group of smaller blue-green trees stood together.

"Your mother will never settle for a tree that small. Besides, you know she likes the Douglas fir better than the Fraser." Scott had told her once that the biggest argument his parents ever had had taken place after a trip with him and his brother to get a Christmas tree.

"I picked up a couple wreaths." He motioned to where two large wreaths decorated with red bows and pine cones sat propped against another tree. "I was thinking this would be a good size for your apartment."

"For me? What would I do with a tree? The last thing I need is a real tree in my apartment. I'm never there. It'd be dead in a week," she said as she handed him his drink. She waited for him to take a swallow.

"It's chocolate," he said as he smacked his mouth.

"Of course it's hot chocolate. We're at a Christmas tree farm." She bent down and picked up one of the wreaths, then waited for him to grab the other.

"Is there some rule that they can't sell coffee at these places?" He gave the drink a suspicious sniff. "I bet if they added some coffee to this, it would be good."

She'd never understood what the man had against chocolate. Of course, it had paid off at Easter when he'd traded his chocolate for her jelly beans, since Leo had always refused to trade with her. "It's delicious and it's warm. Come on. My mom will already have something to say about me not being there to help with the cooking. I don't want to listen to my dad complain about them having to hold dinner for us."

"What about the tree?" he asked, turning back toward the little tree as he picked up the wreaths he had bought earlier.

"If you want to get it for your hotel, buy it. I'm fine without a tree," she said, turning away and heading back to the car. There was no way she was going to let him talk her into taking it home with her. Her apartment was fine just the way it was.

By the time they were back on the road, their earlier conversation had been forgotten and they had returned to comfortable topics. As they pulled into his parents' driveway, she looked down the road where she could just see her own parents' home. When she'd first moved back to the city, she'd made the trip home every weekend she wasn't working. But lately, with the cardiac center nearing its opening, she'd only been able to make it once a month. Her parents had surprised her by encouraging her to stay in the city and assuring her that they were fine without her hovering over them. She'd wanted to point out that she'd learned that talent from the two of them, but hadn't. If the two of them wanted to ignore the fact that they were getting older, that was understandable, but she saw people their age come into the emergency room every day. She couldn't ignore it.

As he parked the car, she started to get out,

then realized that Scott hadn't moved. They both sat and looked at the pink-bricked two-story that had always seemed like a second home to her.

"It's your first time home since…since Leo's death." She didn't know why she felt the need to say it out loud, but she did. Reaching out, she covered his hand with hers, something she wouldn't have dreamed of doing just days ago. They'd agreed to put the past away, but this was different. This loss that the two of them shared went deeper than anything else that had happened in their lives. They couldn't ignore the fact that when they walked into the house, something would be missing.

"Come on," she said as she released his hand. "Your parents are going to be so excited to see you."

CHAPTER FIVE

"Fliss, would you mind going with Scott to take a plate of food down to Ms. Connors for me?" Scott's mother asked as she packed up a plastic container.

Felicity finished drying the last of the large platters that had been used to hold the massive amount of ham that had been served for their Thanksgiving meal as she eyed the container being held out for her to take. It wasn't that she minded running the errand—she had always been fond of her old science teacher— but the fact that throughout the day both her mother and Scott's mother had made a habit of pairing her and Scott together.

But was that really unusual? When Leo had been alive, the three of them had always done things together.

Or was it because things had been strained

between her and Scott since Leo's death that their mothers had decided to get involved? It couldn't be that they knew about what had happened between the two of them in London. No one knew that. No one except the two of them. There was no way Scott had told his mother that they'd ended up in bed together, because if Scott's mother had known, her own mother would have known as soon as the woman could have reached a phone. And then there would have been questions to answer. Lots of questions that she wouldn't have been able to cope with, questions for which she still had no answers.

Realizing she hadn't answered the request, she put down the dish towel and took the container. "Sure. I'll grab my coat and get him."

Walking out of the kitchen, she found Scott in a tall armchair, his eyes shut, though he still held his phone in his hand.

"What?" Scott said, not opening his eyes as she shook his shoulder.

"It's finally happened. You've turned into one of *them*." She motioned to their fathers, both sleeping in a pair of recliners across the room.

Scott opened his eyes and looked over at the two men, then turned his warm hazel eyes back to her as they roamed over her with an intensity that filled her stomach with a warmth that had nothing to do with the hot cider she'd been sipping in the kitchen.

"Nice fashion choice, Mom," he said as he stared at the old floral apron she had forgotten she'd put on.

Yanking it over her head, Felicity pushed both the apron and container of food into his arms before heading to the front door to get bundled up to go out into the cold.

"Your mother needs us to take this over to Ms. Connors's place," she said as she started layering on her sweater and coat.

"Are you sure I should go? Ms. Connors always liked you more than she liked me and Leo," he said as he followed her in getting his own coat on.

"If I'm going, you're going." She opened the door and a cold gust of wind blew into the foyer. "Besides, you need to work off that second piece of pumpkin pie I saw you eat."

"It's snowing again," Scott said as he closed the door behind them.

Big white flakes fell all around them, making her glad she'd worn her sturdy boots as they made their way down the block. The snow was soft and calming as it fell, and the neighborhood was quiet as other families shared their own Thanksgiving meals.

"And why didn't we take the car?" she asked as she wrapped her scarf tighter around her neck and tucked it into her coat as the wind pulled at the strands of hair she had tucked inside her hat.

"You're the one that said I needed to work off the pie. Besides, look around you. It's beautiful. And smell that air." He stopped and took a deep breath as Felicity let herself fill up that need she'd always had to look at him. Being home together was bringing back emotions and memories that made her miss those years when everything had seemed so simple.

But things aren't simple anymore. Everything has changed. We aren't the same people we were before Leo's death. This is how life is now.

She started back up the road. There was nothing good that could come from reliving what had been between the two of them. They both had their own separate lives now, which were thousands of miles apart. They didn't even live on the same continent any longer.

Ms. Connors had always lived in one of the older homes in the neighborhood, but she'd always kept it well maintained and all the children in the neighborhood knew to stay out of her garden. The sound of her voice was enough to put fear into any child or adult. They waited on the small covered front porch for the elderly lady to turn the lock on the door.

"Come in, come in," Ms. Connors said as she led them into a front room where she moved a stack of books to the side, leaving only a small space for the two of them to sit.

"Mom sent you this," Scott said, handing the food container to their former teacher, then taking a seat next to her.

Felicity tried to shift the stack of books farther to the side, only to find them leaning against her until no more than her shoulder kept them in place. Glancing down at the floor, she looked for a place to move them but found yet more stacks leaning precariously against the sofa. She held the opinion that her former teacher had a hoarding problem, which she had once mentioned to Leo, only to be told that having a room overflowing with books was not hoarding. It was called collecting.

She wished her brother were here now to see how the stacks of books had grown. But then maybe he was right. It did seem that the rest of the room was clean and orderly.

She pushed against the stack once more as Scott squeezed farther back into the sofa, leaving her nowhere to escape from the touch of his body against hers.

"We missed you today," she said as she

tried to take her mind off the feel of Scott's warm shoulder against hers.

"I was sorry to miss it, but the weather's just too cold for me to tolerate right now. My arthritis, you know, it acts up every year at this time." Ms. Connors held up a notebook with fingers that looked painfully twisted. "And of course I'm busy working on cataloging all the books I collected while I was teaching."

Looking back around the room, Felicity hoped the woman planned on living a very long life.

"And it's so good to see the two of you together again. Now tell me, what's new with the two of you? I've missed your visits so much. And of course I've missed your brother, Felicity. He was always so good to come by and fill me in on all the gossip from the school."

Felicity felt a deep ache in her heart as she remembered Leo telling her about his visits to the elderly teacher after he had taken a position at their old school.

"He enjoyed those visits as much as you

did. He told me once that your guidance helped him learn his way around all the politics in the school system." Her throat tightened with the words, but she managed to get them out. Felicity always found it hard to talk about her brother, but she knew Leo would want the woman to know how much he had appreciated her.

"Mom said you were thinking about moving," Scott said as he quickly drew the woman into a discussion of the advantages of living closer to her sister.

Thirty minutes later, after listening to Scott describe his job and home in London and respond to the older woman's own memories of once visiting the United Kingdom, Felicity was glad to walk back into the cold. The snow had stopped and left everything blanketed in a thick layer of pristine white.

"Come on," Scott said as he caught her hand and pulled her away from the path that led back to his parents' house.

"What are you doing?" It was only the

warmth of his hand that had her holding on to him.

"Hear that? Everyone's headed to The Hill," Scott said, the laughter in his voice warming her even more. His ability to enjoy the moment was one of the many things she appreciated about him. He always had a knack for having fun wherever he went.

As they turned down a path that led away from the road, the screams of the neighborhood kids got louder. Teenagers shot past them as they raced each other to be the first one down the snowy slope. Scott helped her as they climbed up the back of the hill that was the highest point in the small community, moving to the side as more children ran past them, toting old wooden sleds and brightly colored tire tubes as they all headed to the community park.

At the top of the hill, they stopped and took a breath. The hill was covered in a deep layer of snow and it looked like every kid within ten miles had come to try out the new snowfall. Scott let go of her hand and headed toward two teenage boys.

"How about renting me your sleds? Twenty dollars apiece?" he asked the boys, each holding red wooden sleds that looked as if they had been handed down for generations.

"What are you doing?" He couldn't really think she was going to go down the hill on one of those.

"Just handling a little business deal with these two young men," Scott said before turning back to the boys and pulling out his wallet. "What do you say?"

"You're crazy." And he was very much mistaken if he thought she was going to go along with his plan.

A sharp scream cut through the air from the bottom of the hill and she ran back to the edge, only to find a group of kids engaged in a snowball fight. Both children and adults cried out as they shoved off, sending their sleds and tubes speeding down the hill. Others built snowmen farther down into the park. It was a snowy heaven.

She looked back to where Scott still bargained with the two boys. He turned and motioned her over. Or was it instead a snowy hell?

"I'm not getting on that thing," she said as he handed her one of the sleds. "It's old and rickety. What if it falls apart halfway down the hill?"

"I dare you," Scott said with a wink.

She looked down at the sled in her hand as more screams and laughter floated up from the bottom of the hill. This was stupid, but she had never been one to turn down a dare. "One time down the hill and then I'm done."

Fifteen minutes later she was launching herself down the incline on the flatbed sled and holding on for dear life. She heard Scott's whoop of joy from behind her, and crisp, cold air filled her lungs as her own laughter bubbled out of her. She dived down the hill, feeling as if she were six years old again and this was her first ride.

She saw the bump in the snow right before her sled hit it, sending her airborne for a split second. Then she crashed down into the snow, hurtling even faster toward the bottom of the hill.

She pushed back, extending her feet into the snow as she tried to slow her speed, only to have her sled slide to the right and dump her out beside Scott. Brushing away the icy slush from her face, she took the hand Scott offered and pulled herself up.

"You want to go again?" he asked with a smile that said he already knew her answer.

Grabbing her sled, she took a deep breath of clean, brisk air as Scott had done earlier that day. Happiness flooded through her, and for the first time in forever, she felt the heavy blanket of grief and responsibility lift from her shoulders.

With a squeal she hadn't known she was capable of, she turned and started running back up the hill. "Last one up has to pay for the next ride."

She heard his shout of laughter from behind her as she began the climb back up the hill. It was as if the clock had rewound and things were back to when she and Scott had been the best of friends. It couldn't last, of course. They'd have to go back to the real world soon. But for now, for today, she was going to enjoy this time they had.

Felicity placed the last of her clothes into her weekender bag, then set it off to the side of the bed. It had been a good weekend, spending time with her parents and helping her mother plan the main menu for their Christmas dinner. She hadn't seen Scott since Thursday and she assumed he was spending time with his parents as she was with hers.

Flopping onto her back, she stared up at the ceiling. She had a love-hate relationship with the room. While the bright pink floral curtains and spread from her precollege days were comforting in their familiarity, her grown-up self resented the throwback to a time when she had believed anything was possible. What had happened to that girl? She'd had so many dreams back then. Going to college. Becoming a nurse. Going off to London to work with Scott. And Scott. There had been so many dreams about Scott. And for a moment it had looked like all those dreams would come true.

And then Leo had taken his life and the world she thought she knew had suddenly made no sense. The fact that her parents needed her had kept her strong throughout the first few weeks after losing him, though most of the time she felt as if she was just stumbling from one day to the next. Only later had she been able to ask herself what had happened.

She remembered the last time she'd seen her brother as she'd been about to board the plane to London. He'd told her to be happy as he'd hugged her. She'd seen the sad smile on his face as he waved goodbye from the window after she'd gone through security and she thought it had been because he was going to miss her. But now she knew that there had been more. Had he had the same smile ever since the injury that caused the end of his football career? Had she been so wrapped up in her own life that she hadn't noticed? They'd all known he'd been depressed after his injury, but they'd thought he'd moved past it when he started his teaching job. Why hadn't she been able to see how bad his depression had become? What if leaving had made things worse? What if she had stayed home instead of running away to London to be with Scott? What if she'd stayed home and been there for her brother?

What had she missed? Was there anything she could have done to save him? She would always think that things would have been different if she'd remained near home. She was a nurse. Surely she would have seen some sign that she needed to get help for her brother.

Though she was learning to live her life again, the questions never stopped. And neither did the guilt of knowing the one night her brother had needed her to be there for him, she'd been in the arms of his best friend.

If only she could understand what had happened to her brother. Maybe if she understood why he had taken his life, she would be able to go on living her own. Even with her new job, she felt as if her life was stalled. Her life was suspended in a time known to her as *After Leo's death* versus the vision she'd had for her life in the time *Before Leo's death.*

And now, with her brother's room just feet from her, the memories of all the time they had spent together seemed to be centered here. All around her. Constant and bittersweet in a house that used to bring her comfort and peace.

Her parents had asked if she wanted to help them go through Leo's things, but she hadn't been able to bring herself to do it yet. While she knew it needed to be done, she was too afraid to let go of the past. Too afraid that she'd lose her brother's memory if she let the past go. And the guilt? How could she let that go when she knew things would have been different for all of them if she'd been there for him?

Something hit the bedroom window and she jerked to attention. It wouldn't be a bird this late at night. Before she could get to the window, something knocked against it. It couldn't be, could it?

She raised the shade. Scott's face was only visible with the light of the full moon. The window creaked as she slid it up and she stopped, afraid she'd wake her parents.

Shaking her head with disgust, she finished opening the window. She was acting like a teenage girl, afraid her parents would ground her for sneaking a boy into her room. She stood back so that the *boy* sneaking into her room could climb through the window.

"What are you doing here?" Her mind went to several reasons he could be climbing into her window, most having to do with the bed that occupied the room.

"I wanted to talk," Scott said as he looked around the room.

"You lost your phone? You forgot where our front door was located? You just felt adventurous and wanted to take a chance getting shot by my dad?" she asked. "What possible reason could you have for climbing that ladder in the dark? You could have fallen to your death."

"I didn't want to wake your parents," Scott said. "Come on. I want to show you something."

"Not even I am naive enough to fall for that line." Her heart hammered against her chest as his lips turned up in a smile of which any wolf would be proud. What had she been thinking letting him into her room? "Okay, Doc. What's up?"

"Just trust me," he said as he began climbing back out the window.

"You know you're crazy, right?" she asked as she climbed out behind him, not daring to look down. Not that she hadn't used this same ladder herself to get in and out of the house when she was younger, much younger than she was now. The frosty cold air filled her lungs and bit into her skin the moment she stepped onto the ladder.

"Wait. I need my coat." She reached back inside the window and pulled it off the chair where she had laid it.

Backing down the ladder slowly, she stumbled on a step and Scott's hand shot out to steady her, then remained on her back, leaving her feeling anything but steady.

She climbed into his car, then laughed when he turned on the engine but didn't turn the lights on until they had pulled out of her parents' driveway. "What are we? Sixteen?"

"I have a reputation to uphold, you know," he said as he turned back toward the highway that would take them out of town.

As he took the next right, she realized where he was taking her. She was suddenly aware that she wore only a pair of button-up pajamas under her coat. "Getting caught at Make-Out Lake is not going to help that reputation you're so worried about."

"The kids probably don't even call it that anymore. And I'm pretty sure taking a drive out to *Stone Lake* is probably not going to get me in trouble," he said. His eyes never left the road, but she could see the smirk on his face. He was probably remembering all those nights he'd sneaked out to the lake with his high school dates. That thought made her stomach tighten with her old friend the green-eyed monster again.

But she knew she didn't have any right to feel that way. She'd put her romantic feelings for Scott aside. There was no future there and she wasn't going to waste her energy on something that could not be.

They turned off the road that led to the lake and took a path that was just wide enough for a car. In the headlights she could see the outline of trees, but it wasn't until they came out of the dark woods that she could see the lake itself.

The full moon reflected off the still body of water, giving the whole lakefront a magical glow as snow piles carpeted the trees, twinkling like fairy lights as the branches swayed in with the winter breeze.

"It's beautiful," she whispered, not wanting to spoil the moment. Everything seemed so peaceful here. It was as if the whole world was frozen in place.

Just as your life has been frozen in place.

She shivered as that truth settled around her.

"It is very beautiful." Scott had known when he'd driven down here earlier that evening that he needed to share this with Fliss. But did she see what he saw? "It's so peaceful, yet at the same time I'm afraid to breathe because it looks so fragile."

He didn't say that it was the same way he felt about their friendship. That he was afraid to say too much, to feel too much, because of the fragile new beginning that had finally emerged over the weekend.

But some things did need to come out in the open if they were going to have any chance of a future relationship, though he regretted the pain he knew that it could cause the two of them.

"Your parents are worried about you." He waited for the explosion that he had expected from her for inserting himself in her affairs, but it didn't come. Instead she just stared out into the dark as if he hadn't spoken.

"I called him about us," Scott said, surprising even himself with his words. It wasn't as if he had ever intended to keep it to himself. He just hadn't had a chance to discuss things privately with her before the funeral. And afterward, when she had told him she wasn't returning to London with him, there hadn't seemed to be any reason to bring it up to her.

"What do you mean?" Her voice was quiet, but there was a tension in her body that hadn't been there earlier.

"The night before our first real date, I called him. I had to, Fliss. It wouldn't have been right to have him find out any other way. I owed it to him."

"You make it sound like the two of you were going to face off at dawn over pistols. Leo loved you, Scott. He would never have been mad at you."

Scott was glad to see that some of the tension between them was gone, but there was still so much for them to discuss.

"What did he say?" she asked, her voice once again quiet, as if she wasn't sure she wanted to hear the answer.

"You mean after he cussed me like a dog and pretended to warn me off?" He smiled at the memory of the colorful words his friend had used.

"He didn't seem surprised, really. He told me to take good care of you and he threatened my life if I broke your heart." And hadn't that been a bit hypocritical of his friend when only days later he had broken both Scott's and Fliss's hearts?

"He seemed…okay, then?" she asked, then shivered.

He turned the heat up in the car. The snow had begun to fall again and the temperatures outside were dropping.

He'd gone over his conversation with Leo word by word and there hadn't been any sign that his friend was depressed. He'd seemed happy and upbeat just like he had always been when Scott talked to him. Only now Scott knew that it had all been an act. His friend had to have been suffering to do something as drastic as taking his own life.

"Yes. He seemed happy with the news. There was nothing he said that even hinted he was depressed."

"You know, he didn't seem surprised when we became closer friends after he went off to college. I've always wondered if he had anything to do with that." She had turned toward him now and the light from the moon that lit the sky shone across the light blond hair that cascaded down her back. Her eyes, turned up toward his, shone with a sapphire light all their own. She was as beautiful as the landscape outside.

"He might have suggested that I keep an eye on you, but that was all," he said. Then, without thinking, he pulled her close so that her head rested on his shoulder. "It's still hard to believe he's gone. I think of picking up the phone and calling him whenever the Yankees bite the dust, and then I remember he's not here anymore."

"It's not fair," she said, her voice steady, though he could feel the dampness of her tears through his shirt.

"It never is." The truth of the words hit him hard. It wasn't fair that he'd lost both Leo and Fliss at the same time either.

What if they'd had this conversation before? What if he had demanded she let him help her through this grief before she locked him out of her thoughts and emotions? What if they'd worked through Leo's death together?

The what-ifs were piling up like the snow outside the car. There was no going back to the way things had been before Leo's death, but they both could move forward as friends again. His body's own reaction to her nearness protested against that thought. He couldn't lie to himself. He wanted more than friendship, but he would be glad to take what he could get right now because the time they'd spent together this weekend had given him hope that there could be more between them someday.

"My parents have no reason to worry about me. I'm doing great. The new job in New York is more than I could have hoped for." She moved away as she spoke, then turned back toward him. "I'm excited to see everything we've worked for put into action. Not only is it going to make a difference to the way the whole cardiac department is run, it's going to free up space in the ER for other patients."

There was no denying the excitement in her eyes. The only time she really seemed like her old self, the happy Fliss he'd grown up with, was when she talked about her work. The only other time he had seen that look in her eyes had been when she'd been flying down the hill on the sled he'd rented.

"Can you just do me one favor before we leave? I never… I mean, when we were growing up, I didn't get to…" she said as he started to put the car into Reverse. "Can you just kiss me before we leave?"

Putting the car back in Park, he tensed as she undid her seat belt and moved closer.

"I know it sounds stupid, but…"

His lips sealed over hers before she could say anything more. It had been so long, too long, since he'd tasted her. What had brought on her request, he didn't care.

Her lips opened to his and his hands tangled in her hair as he swept inside her mouth, his tongue beginning an intimate dance with hers, touching, retreating, then tangling together.

She pulled away from him, her lips as bright red from his kisses as the color that filled her cheeks. Only the binding of the seat belt kept him from following her to her side of the car. Her chest rose and fell with the same desperate need for air that he was experiencing. He wasn't the only one shaken by what they had just shared.

"What I was going to say was that I never had the chance to be kissed at Make-Out Lake and I always felt like I had missed out on one of those teenage milestones." She straightened her clothes, then buckled her seat belt.

He knew this was true because all the boys in her classes had been warned off by both him and her brother.

He decided it was time to leave before he got it into his mind to educate her on all the other things that had gone on at their high school make-out spot. Just thinking about doing them with Fliss made the drive back to her parents' home very uncomfortable.

He waited while she lifted a small pot in her mother's garden for a hidden key, then went inside the house.

Driving away, he couldn't help but hope that there was some way the passionate woman who had been in his arms for just those few moments, the one he had fallen for in London, would somehow find her way back to him before it was too late and they were separated again.

CHAPTER SIX

SCOTT GLANCED OVER to where Felicity slept in her seat next to him. From the few grunts she'd made since he had picked her up and started driving back to the city, it was obvious that she hadn't slept much better than he had.

Unable to forget the feel of her lips against his, he'd spent the night wondering how they had managed to mess things up between them so quickly. Yes, Leo's death changed both of their lives forever. But shouldn't that have been even more of a reason to turn to each other?

Even when she sent him away, he'd not believed that she meant for it to be permanent. She just needed some time to deal with the loss of her brother before she could return to London.

But when six months had passed and she still wouldn't talk to him, he had let his pride get the best of him. Instead of flying to New York and demanding that Felicity talk to him, he'd accepted that not only had he lost Leo, but he'd lost her too. He could see that had been a mistake.

Now those old what-ifs had wound their way back into his subconscious, as they had after Leo's death, until they had worn a path so deep that he couldn't seem to get away from them. Like Felicity, it had only been his work that had pulled him from the abyss. But he'd realized over the last few months that it wasn't enough anymore.

And just one taste of Felicity had shown him that he wanted more. He wanted the future that he had glimpsed for just a few wonderful moments. He wanted the woman he had fallen in love with in London.

He saw the sign for the Christmas tree farm that they'd stopped at earlier in the week and an idea formed in his head. He missed the happy, spontaneous woman who had lit up his world. And that woman had always loved Christmas. His mother had told him there was magic in Christmas if you only believed in it. He was pretty sure that Fliss had lost the ability to believe in anything. But maybe he could believe enough for the two of them.

He turned the car into the parking lot. Somehow he knew that helping Fliss find the magic of Christmas again was the key to her also finding herself and moving on with her life. Maybe then she would find her way back to him.

Felicity woke at the slamming of the car door. Scrambling up in the seat, she looked around her and was surprised to see that they were once again at a Christmas tree farm. No, not *a* Christmas farm—it was the same one they had stopped at before. Dragging her coat and scarf on, she went to look for Scott, only to find him waiting in line while a young boy tied twine around a small tree much like the one he'd admired before.

"I hope you're not buying that for me," she

said as she followed the two of them to the car, where they worked on tying it to the luggage rack on the roof.

"I know it's a little small, but it should fit perfectly by the fireplace," Scott said as he checked the knots holding the tree in place.

"I told you before, I don't need a tree. I'm hardly ever home. It's just a waste." And when had he picked out a place for it in her apartment? He'd only been inside once, the day they'd left for the weekend. "Look, it's sweet of you to think of it, but seriously, I don't need it."

"Of course you do. And don't worry about decorations. I'll pick some up for it."

Had he always been this high-handed? Or had that kiss, the one she was trying hard to forget, given him the wrong idea? Why had she done it? Was it because she had spent so many nights lying in her bed, knowing that Scott and Leo were out at the lake with their girlfriends while she was home alone, secretly wishing she'd been the one Scott had chosen? She had to admit that his kiss had been even better than the ones her imagination had dreamed of. All of their kisses had been better than her imagined ones. Her mind flashed back to the night they'd spent together. Her lips. His lips. Everywhere.

She loosened the knot of her scarf, hoping to let the icy air in to cool her skin. She was not going to think about it. It was in the past, where it needed to stay.

Refusing to argue the point with him any longer, she climbed back into the car. He might have insisted on buying it, but that didn't mean she had to accept it.

Thirty minutes later she couldn't bite her tongue any longer. "Why is it so important to you that I have a tree?"

"It's Christmastime, Fliss. You've always had a tree. It's not the first tree we've picked out together. Don't you remember the lot we went to in London?" he asked. "The poor thing couldn't have been three feet tall."

"And it still barely fit in the living room." It had been more of a bush than a tree, but it had held a small string of lights and enough balls to qualify as a Christmas tree. After they'd finished decorating, they'd gorged themselves on popcorn and watched a lineup of British Christmas movies. She'd been homesick for her family during the holiday season, but that night Scott had made her feel like she was at home. He'd taken care of her then just like he was trying to take care of her now.

How could she explain to him that, to her, Christmas was just one more day to get through now? "I do appreciate the thought. I just don't think I'm ready for it this year."

"Whether you're ready or not, Christmas is coming," Scott said as he moved his hand over hers where it rested on the console.

"You've moved on with your life." She didn't mean the words as an accusation. She was just stating a painful fact that she found hard to understand.

"Would you rather I hadn't?" he asked.

Would she rather he still be mourning her brother? It embarrassed her that her first thought was that she wished he hadn't moved on. Because she wanted him to be just as miserable as she was? No, not really. It was the fear that Leo would be forgotten if they all went on with their lives.

"It doesn't mean I've forgotten him, Fliss. I never will." That his words were so tuned to her thoughts didn't surprise her. It had always been that way between the two of them.

"Spend Christmas with me," he said.

"I have to be at my parents' for Christmas. They'll need me. You know that. Besides, your parents will be there too." She wasn't sure what Scott was planning, but she knew it frightened her.

"Not the day. The season. Let me show you that you can still enjoy Christmas." His words held so much hope.

"Scott, if I gave you the wrong idea by asking you to kiss me, I'm sorry." It was important that they didn't have any misunderstandings between them. They still had a professional relationship that they had to return to the next day.

"No expectations. Just two old friends enjoying the Christmas season together," Scott said as he pulled his hand away from hers, and the cozy comfort of the car that she had been enjoying seemed to disappear. "For old times' sake?"

How could she turn down his offer when she knew all he wanted to do was help?

"Okay, Doc. I'll go along with this plan of yours." She'd take the tree and agree to some shopping if it would get him to change the subject. "Now turn those hazel eyes of yours back to the road and concentrate on getting us back to the city. Vacation time is over. Tomorrow it's back to work for the both of us."

It was the smell of paint that drove her into Scott's office the next day. Well, technically it was her office. At least, it would be when Scott returned to London. Moving a small table that she had originally planned to use for organizing file folders, she set up an area for her laptop and the stack of envelopes and invitations that she had started addressing after her lunch meeting.

"There you are," Scott said as he came into the office. "I'm glad you finally joined me."

"What do you mean?" He made it sound like she had been avoiding him. Of course, that was what she had been doing when he'd first arrived. She'd surrendered her office to him without a single complaint. It had seemed like the best thing for both of them while things had been so tumultuous between them.

"I didn't mean to throw you out of the office. Like I told you before, it's big enough for the two of us to share, I would think." He began to move his folders and papers as he cleaned off a spot on the desk.

"Until the painters finish in the lounge, we will definitely be sharing, but I'm quite happy over here. There's plenty of room for what I need." She studied the list she had made of hospital board members and medical officers who would be invited to the grand opening that would take place in just two weeks' time.

"Did you have a chance to review the list of invited guests?" Though she knew he wasn't familiar with most of the people in the hospital, she didn't want to leave off anyone Dr. Mason might have mentioned wanting to invite.

"I did and I ran it by Dr. Mason at our meeting this morning. He was happy to see that you had included some of the vendors. It's always good to keep a good relationship in the community, especially when they go into other hospitals," Scott said.

"Dr. Mason just wants to spread the word about the program, I'm sure." And make sure that all his colleagues in the city ended up green with envy at what he had been able to accomplish with the new center.

A knock came on the door, and Theresa, one of the new charge nurses who had volunteered to help unpack supplies, stuck her head into the room.

"I've finished stocking the nurses' station, but I wanted to see if you wanted to join some of us from the ER. It's tree-lighting day at the Rockefeller Center, you know." The words bubbled out of the woman and Felicity couldn't ignore the way she was staring hopefully at Scott. "I know you're from upstate New York, Dr. Thomas, but I wasn't sure if you knew about the lighting."

"Felicity and I have attended the lighting several times," Scott said. "If we missed the lighting, Fliss would insist that we stop by the tree at least once while we were in the city during the holidays."

She wasn't certain whether he had purposely brought her into the conversation to cool down the woman's interest in him or whether he was just being friendly.

"Really?" the woman asked, glancing over at Felicity with a look of disbelief.

Was it possible that there was one person left in the hospital who wasn't aware that she and Scott were old friends?

"I'm sorry, Theresa, but I really need to finish these invitations, or we'll have a very lonely grand opening." She went back to work on the invitations. If Scott wanted to go with the other woman, she wasn't going to stand in his way. It wasn't like she needed his help to finish with this project.

"I'd love to, but I've got a few charts to sign off after my shift in the cath lab before I leave tonight. But thanks for the invite. Maybe next time," Scott said.

The possibility of him attending the ceremony with her another year seemed to satisfy the woman as she hurried out the door with a smile on her face. Felicity didn't mention that next time the famous Christmas tree was lit he'd be halfway around the world.

And where would she be next Christmas? Working these same late shifts just to have something to help pass the long, lonely hours? Okay, now she was just being maudlin.

Minutes ticked by as they both worked quietly. While addressing envelopes wasn't what she'd dreamed of when she'd taken the new position, it was a bit exciting to see the stack of invitations pile up. There was a lot of pressure coming down from administration for this grand opening to go well, especially with the board members planning to attend.

But the real excitement would be when the unit was finally open to the community. Getting the word out that there was a fast track through the emergency room that would increase the survival chances of a patient with a cardiac emergency was just as important as showing the unit off to the bigwigs of the hospital.

"Let's do it!" Scott said, startling her.

"Do what?" she asked as she straightened a stack of envelopes she had knocked over.

"Let's go to the tree lighting. You always loved it when the three of us got to be there," Scott said. "I can come in early and finish the few charts I have left."

She didn't bother to tell him that it wasn't the three of them anymore. He had to realize it wouldn't be the same without Leo. He knew she avoided everything that reminded her of her brother. She looked at her phone where it lay beside her. "It's too late. We'd never make it through traffic now."

"We can take a car service and..." His phone rang, interrupting him. It was clear there was some type of emergency.

"There's a patient coming by air. The crew

called in a STEMI, but then the patient lost his pulse. If they can get him back, they want to go straight to the cath lab, but Dr. Turner is tied up with another emergency." Scott grabbed his go bag that she knew contained a fresh pair of scrubs.

"I'm going to meet them on the roof with the ER staff."

"I'll make sure the lab is ready. I can assist if needed. Just call and let me know if you're coming straight over." She grabbed the shoes she had kicked off under the table earlier.

"Will do," Scott said, running out the door.

Heading out of the office, she stopped for a second and admired the shiny new nurses' station. This was why this unit was important. If they'd been open, the patient would have been able to come straight here, where they would work to stabilize him before taking him to the cath lab next door.

Fifteen minutes later she stood at the control booth and watched as Scott inserted an intra-aortic balloon pump. She'd watched on the monitors as he opened up the blocked artery that had likely been the cause of the man's MI, but she knew the damage to the man's heart was extensive if Scott was having to put him on the device that would help his heart continue to work.

"The man's a miracle," said the technologist in charge of the monitors and documentation.

"Not many survive the widow-maker," she said, referring to the man's blockage in his main coronary artery.

"I'm not sure this guy is going to survive, but at least we've given him a chance now. I mean, Dr. Thomas. There's something about his technique that makes it all look so simple," the man said before turning back to his monitors.

The pride she felt at the compliment on Scott's behalf was the same she'd felt when they'd been working together in London and she would overhear comments on the special ability he had to make his procedures go off so easily for the staff and the patient.

That time in London seemed so long ago now, though she did think about it often.

There'd been a certain magic to the city with the charm of its history and people. But that was a lifetime ago, and there was no reason for her to relive those memories now. She was glad she had them—most of the time—but she knew she'd made the right decision to stay with her parents.

She turned away from the monitors and headed back to the office. There was a lot of work left to do before she could finish for the night.

CHAPTER SEVEN

SCOTT WAS HAPPY to find Felicity back in what hopefully would now become *their* office. He knew they were both tired, but the last case had drained him more emotionally than physically. He didn't feel like going back to the hotel by himself. Not yet, at least. "You ready to go?" Scott asked as he gathered his own laptop into his briefcase.

"I was just heading out," she said. "How did it go with the wife?"

"It's always hard to tell someone's loved ones that the patient might not make it. They have a set of twins away in college. She was calling them when I left her with the chaplain." He knew he'd done everything he could for the man, but it didn't make it any easier to watch the wife break down when he told her she needed to call their daughters so they could be here if their father didn't survive the night.

"Let's go. We have an appointment," he said as he shut the office door behind them.

The look she gave him was not a surprise. Of course, Fliss had never liked surprises. It was the reason her family had refused to put out her Christmas presents even after she was too old to believe in Santa Claus. She'd been caught red-handed more than once with a half-unwrapped present.

"Have you forgotten the breakfast meeting with Dr. Mason in the morning?" she asked.

"It's not that late," he said as they stepped out of the side entrance that led to the parking lots. He spotted the car with his hotel's insignia across its door. He just hoped the concierge had been able to arrange the rest of his last-minute request. Taking her arm, Scott guided her through the other cars that waited for their fares.

"You know we've already missed the tree lighting, right? And I really do need to get home. Maybe you don't need your beauty sleep, but some of us do," Felicity said as she scooted over in the back seat for him to climb in next to her and began to give her address to the driver.

"I just had to tell a woman that her husband might not make it through the night. Life's short, Fliss. You have to make time for more than work," Scott said as he laid a hand on her arm. "Just go with me on this one. Please?"

He waited as she considered his request, finally relaxing when she settled back into the car seat as she made sure there was plenty of space between the two of them so they weren't touching. He hoped the space would be gone by the time the evening was over.

They rode in silence, Fliss undoubtedly trying to figure out what he could have planned for the night. Sitting back, he let himself enjoy the view of the city that seemed even more alive now that darkness had fallen. Lights of every color shone from the small businesses that lined the street as they prepared for the coming holidays. Looking up into the sky, he could see the larger buildings whose lights always made up the backdrop of the city. It was truly The City That Never Sleeps. And he loved everything about it.

When the car stopped, he made arrangements with the driver to return, then took Felicity's hand. "This way."

He waited for her reaction when she reluctantly exited the car. The smile she gave him more than compensated for the lack of sleep from which the two of them would be suffering the next morning.

"You've always said that one day you wanted to take a carriage ride through the city." He didn't have to say how corny the whole carriage in Central Park had seemed when he was a young teenager. He'd been afraid that she was going to force him and Leo to take a ride with her. Now he couldn't wait to take this ride with her. Looking at the wonder and happiness he could see in her eyes, he knew he'd take a carriage ride up the entire East Coast if it made her this happy.

"Which one do we take?" she asked. "Can

we take the one with that big black horse? The one with the white carriage?"

"Let's find out." Still holding her hand, he pulled her along with him till they came to the beautiful black mare that stood with its driver at the front of the line. Minutes later they were loaded inside and headed down the path out of Central Park.

As he tucked the blankets in around her, Felicity moved closer till their shoulders touched, the movement more instinct and habit than intentional, he was sure. He had missed the warmth of her on those cold nights in London.

There had been so many changes to their relationship after she had come to London. The longtime companionship he had enjoyed with her had quickly turned into something more. He had enjoyed each new experience as their relationship had changed, becoming more intimate and deeper than anything he had felt before. It was as if they had discovered something new about each other every day as they explored their new romantic interest in each other.

And explore they had. They'd spent many nights talking for hours in their favorite English pub. And then there had been the even longer good-nights at her door until finally he'd gotten the nerve to make the move for that first good-night kiss. Just one kiss and he'd known things would never be the same between them. When she'd sighed into his mouth and opened her lips for him, he'd known there was no going back. Never again could he look at his best friend without thinking of the sweet taste of her lips.

It was the kiss that had had him waking Leo up with the call he'd known he had to make immediately. While the two of them had taken different paths after high school, they had still remained close and he didn't want anything to endanger their friendship. The fact that Leo hadn't been surprised that there had been changes in his sister's relationship with his old friend just showed how well he knew the two of them. And with Leo's blessing, he'd had the courage to explore this new connection with Fliss.

If he had only known what the future held for the three of them then.

"Look, you can see the lights from the Saks window display." Felicity moved closer as she pointed down the street to their destination. Sally, the black draft horse pulling their carriage, clopped slowly down the street as Felicity bounced up and down beside him as if she could help the horse go faster.

Putting his arm around her, he pulled her close. The smell of honeysuckle hit him, reminding him of the bottle of shampoo that still sat in his shower where she'd left it the morning they'd flown out of London.

"Relax. The store's not going to go anywhere. You don't want to spook the horse." He pulled her closer against him. It was probably wrong of him to use the poor horse as an excuse to hold her.

While there were still plenty of people on the streets, they had a good view of the store as thousands of color-coordinated lights ran up and down the building. The driver slowed the carriage and Scott pulled his phone out to take a picture of Felicity's face as she took in all the lights. He'd send it to her mother the next day.

When the tree at Rockefeller Center came into view, they both moved up in the seat. The lighting of a tree was a long-held tradition for the city and it seemed that each year the tree got more spectacular.

"Do you remember the first time we came to see the tree?" Felicity asked.

"I remember it was cold. Too cold for anyone with any sense to be outside." Both he and her brother had complained about the trip, only going with her because she had insisted she would go alone if they didn't come.

"And you and Leo whined about it the whole time we were here. It was New York in the winter. It was supposed to be cold. What I remember is how excited the crowd was when we were counting down. Then when the tree lit up and the choir started singing, it was magical." She sat back in the seat, her face lit with a smile.

"It is still magical," he said as he looked

down into her eyes. If only she could see the magic that still surrounded the two of them. He bent his head to hers before he could think too hard about what he was doing and brushed his lips across hers, letting them linger there for just a moment. It wasn't much more than a peck on the lips, but he knew he was playing with fire when for a mere second her lips opened and he enjoyed the taste of her before she pulled away. He saw the uncertainty in her eyes before she turned her face away from him. His heart stuttered for a beat as if it knew it was in danger. Fliss had broken it when she'd sent him back to London alone, and there was no reason to doubt that she would do it again. But was it possible for them to at least have these next few weeks together? If this were all he could ever have of her, would he take it?

She turned back to the lights of the street as if nothing had happened between them. Had he just ruined what he had been so carefully building between the two of them? Would one kiss, one night, one Christmas together be enough for him?

They turned the corner and St. Patrick's Cathedral came into view, its Gothic architecture always awe-inspiring. As they left the crowded streets and headed back to Central Park, the rest of the trip was spent in silence as they both seemed occupied with their own thoughts.

By the time they returned to the cab, they both were dragging from the length of the day. As the car drove the two of them back toward the hospital, he was relieved when Fliss leaned against him once more.

"I'm glad we're friends again," she said as she closed her eyes.

It wasn't much—and definitely not the declaration he had hoped for—but for now it would have to do. They'd come a long way, but they still had far to go.

Felicity glanced around her small apartment to make sure once more that everything was in place. Agreeing to Scott's request that he bring over decorations for the tree he had insisted on buying her, she'd had to rush home to straighten up before he arrived. Now, dressed in a soft pair of jeans and a warm sweater, she stood in the middle of her small apartment and found herself thinking about the times Scott had hung out in her even smaller flat in London. With a kitchen too small to do any real cooking, she'd lived on takeout, until one night when she'd decided to cook a meal for Scott. It had been a disaster from the moment she'd put the small chicken in the tiny oven to the moment the fire alarm in the building had gone off. As usual, Scott had pitched in and helped with the cleanup without commenting on the fact that she was a disaster in the kitchen. Instead he'd picked up the phone and ordered takeout, acting as if that had been the plan all along. Of course, since he'd experienced her cooking before, it might have been.

She hadn't thought much of her apartment in London recently. Or at least she had tried not to think of it. She'd left it so suddenly.

Her thoughts at the time had only been for her parents. It wasn't until after the funeral that she'd known she couldn't return to London. Her parents had been too fragile at the time. She'd made the hardest decision of her life in a matter of hours, knowing that if she took too long to think about it, she might not be able to do what she knew was best for all of them. She'd had to stay with her parents. And she'd had to let Scott go to live out his dream of working in London. After seeing where her brother's failure to achieve his dream had taken him, she couldn't be responsible for Scott's dream ending because of her.

Her apartment doorbell buzzed, and checking the camera, she opened the door for Scott, who carried two large boxes.

"That seems a bit much for such a little tree, don't you think?" She took the top box from him, then placed it on the small kitchen table. When a whiff of ginger and garlic met her nose, she opened the box, revealing multiple small cartons. "You remembered?"

"That we always vetoed your request of

Chinese and substituted pizza and beer when we decorated the tree?" He laid the other box next to the tree, then took off his coat. "It wasn't really fair using our two-guy votes against you all the time."

It had been enough to make her scream at times when her brother and Scott sided against her, but she'd eat all the pizza in the world if things could go back to the way they were then.

"Besides, it's time for some new traditions. And I'm starving," he said as he moved the pizza takeout menus on the table out of the way.

They ate in silence, as they both had missed lunch due to a last-minute meeting called by the hospital plant operations department, who had felt the need to discuss the new fire security doors that had been added during construction.

"I know this sounds crazy, but I can't wait till I'm back to taking care of simple things like a patient having an MI," she said, then laughed. "I guess that sounds heartless. I don't mean I want someone to die. I'm just tired of all these people in suits thinking that the color of the tile in the staff bathroom needs five meetings and six pages of reports filled out."

"I know exactly what you mean. All the bureaucracy can be hard to deal with," said Scott, "but in the end you'll see that it's been worth it. Brooklyn Heights is going to be the talk of the cardiac community once the new unit opens up."

"Don't you miss working with your patients in London?" She waited for his answer, knowing he would never lie to her. Why did she feel the need to know that sending him away before had been the right thing to do? It didn't matter now.

"London is spectacular. You know that," he said.

The fact that he didn't say more confused her. He'd always been so excited about his job with the cardiac team at the prestigious hospital in London.

"And your job?" she asked, pushing for more.

"I love the job. The hospital is state of the art in its cardiac department and the staff is phenomenal, as you know," Scott said, then turned toward the box he had brought with him. "I know you prefer white lights, but these just seemed right for this space."

He pulled out a small string of blue mini lights. "I have another string of white ones in here in case you don't like these. And I also picked these up."

He pulled out another box, then took out a small ornament and handed it to her. Holding the crystal snowflake up to the light, she watched as prisms of all the colors of the rainbow danced across the bare walls of her apartment.

"They're beautiful." She carefully placed it down, then reached for the string of blue lights. "Let's put them on."

In minutes the tree was quickly transformed into a spectacular winter arrangement. The pale blue of the lights reflected off the ornaments and walls, turning the small room into a winter wonderland that brought back the memory of their trip to their parents' homes.

"It's perfect," she said as she sat back and admired the small tree. Scott's choices had transformed it from a small forgotten bush in the corner of the room to the room's centerpiece. "How do you always seem to know what something needs?"

Or what I need?

It had always been that way with him. He consistently seemed to know what she needed and exactly when she needed it. In high school, he'd known when she needed that bit of encouragement to step out of her comfort zone. In college, she could always count on him for a phone call right when she was feeling overwhelmed with exams and clinicals. Sometimes it had seemed that he knew her better than even her brother or her parents. It was like he knew what she needed before even she did.

And then there was this little tree that seemed to drive out some of the gloom that had settled over her lonely apartment. It was perfect.

"Wait," she said as she jumped up from where they sat around the tree and ran toward the front door. She flipped the switch to both the living room and kitchen. The room went dark except for the pretty pale lights of the tree.

"Now it's perfect," she said as she took her place in front of the tree. Minutes passed as they both just watched the lights and their reflection in the crystal snowflakes, but there was no awkwardness in this silence. Instead the moment was one of shared peacefulness. The crowded streets of the city and Scott's hospital back in London were both thousands of miles away right then. For now there was just the two of them with this brightly lit Christmas tree and it was enough. And if a little bit of Christmas spirit eased its way into her heart, she wasn't about to admit it to him.

CHAPTER EIGHT

"WE COULD HAVE just driven over to the mall," Felicity grumbled. They had agreed to make an early morning start, which would have been fine except for the fact that she hadn't slept more than a couple of hours the night before. She wanted to blame the Chinese food, but knew it was more than that. She'd spent a long time in front of her newly decorated tree after Scott had left, going over all her memories of past Christmases that she'd spent with both Scott and Leo. She'd been able to block out all those memories the year before, but this Christmas season was different.

Because of Scott. He was forcing her into the present, but all she wanted was to keep looking back at the past. It seemed better to look back to the past than to think about the future.

"But you've always loved shopping the market fair. You think Dad would like this?" Scott asked as he picked up a small carving of a sailboat.

"It's nice, but I like that one better." She pointed to the slightly larger one that reminded her more of Scott's father's boat.

"Nice." Scott picked it up and examined it. "I like the sail work on it."

"I'll take it," he said as he handed it to the salesperson.

"See, this is why I need you," he said as he turned toward her. "You have this great knack for picking out the perfect gift."

"Are you talking about that awful sweater you were going to buy your mother? Anyone could have told you that was all wrong. What woman is going to wear a sweater with a huge sequined fish?" It had truly been the worst sweater she had ever seen.

"I thought it was cute," Scott said as he paid and they moved on. He stopped at a small jewelry shop that had been set up temporarily in Grand Central.

How a man who had picked out and decorated her Christmas tree so perfectly could think that sweater was cute was impossible for her to understand. Of course, his gifts had always been more quirky than traditional.

She spotted a nice light green crocheted afghan that she knew her mother would love. She held it up to the light. Each stitch was precise and the yarn was a soft wool. She was handing it to the salesperson when Scott walked up with a jewelry bag in his hand. She wanted to ask him what he'd bought but stopped herself. What if it was for someone back in London? A woman? Was it possible he had someone waiting for him in London? He'd certainly had his share in both high school and med school. It shouldn't have been a surprise to her if there was someone in his life now.

And the kiss they'd shared the night of the carriage ride? She'd assured him that it had only been a kiss between friends, but it had felt like more. So had the kiss at the lake.

"I'm starved. Do you want to get something to eat?" he asked. "How about lunch at Macy's? I know you wanted to shop for some new ties for your dad."

She forced herself to smile and nodded her head, unable to think of anything but what the small jewelry bag in his hand could contain while he sent out a request for the car service.

She was being ridiculous. It only made sense that Scott would have a woman in his life. It had been over eighteen months since their breakup—if you could call ending a relationship that had lasted one night a breakup.

But wouldn't he tell her if there was someone else? Over the last couple of weeks, they had been finding that close friendship that they had enjoyed for most of their lives. Wouldn't he at least have shared something about a new woman in his life? And there was still that kiss. It was hard to believe he would have kissed her, even as a friend, if he'd been involved with someone else.

By the time she was taking a seat at the small restaurant inside Macy's, she knew she had to know if there was a woman. Not that it would really make a difference in their relationship. As a friend, she had no right to anything he didn't want to share with her.

She managed to wait until after the waitress had taken their orders before trying to bring up the subject. She didn't want to appear too interested or to cross some line that would make it uncomfortable for the two of them to continue with the new friendship they had managed to find.

"You haven't said much about London. Tell me all the gossip," she said, trying to play it off as a natural interest in her former coworkers. She immediately thought of a brown-eyed beauty that had made it clear to Felicity from day one that she had an interest in Scott.

No. There was no way he could have fallen for Katie. He was too intelligent to get involved with a woman who made it clear that she was husband-shopping for the man with the biggest wallet.

And that didn't sound jealous at all. Nope. Not one bit.

"There's not a lot of gossip to tell you about. Dr. Matthews is getting a divorce. You were the one who pointed out all the signs to me, if I remember correctly. The poor guy is dating Katie Callahan now." Scott took a drink of his water while she silently celebrated this news.

"I'm not surprised by the divorce, but I am about Katie." Dr. Matthews was a nice guy, but if Katie was the type of woman he wanted, then she would wish the two of them the best of luck.

"There's no explanation for some people's taste." Their drinks came, along with an appetizer of crispy oven-roasted vegetables. Her mouth could all but taste the cauliflower and pine nuts, but her stomach was still filled with nerves.

She served herself and then pushed the vegetables around on her plate. This wasn't the way she did things—at least, not with Scott. They'd always been able to talk about everything. She'd even been known to give him advice on women, even though the cost had been high to her own morale. There was no reason, if they were going to be friends, that they couldn't talk about their involvement with other people. She was just going to have to face this square on. She could do it. She'd listened to him talk about other women in his life before, so what was the difference now?

Maybe the fact that for a very short time she'd been the woman in his life? Her heart squeezed as tight as a fist at the memory.

This wasn't working. She needed to just come out and ask him.

"Scott, are you dating anyone?" The question sounded ridiculous now that she'd voiced it. Did she sound like a jealous ex-lover? If Scott had wanted to tell her about someone in his life, he would have done so.

He slowly lowered his glass without taking his eyes from hers. "Why would you ask that?"

"It just seems… I mean… I'm sorry. I know it's none of my business." She took a swallow from her own glass.

"Do you think I'm the kind of guy that would kiss another woman when I was in a relationship with someone else? After all these years, after everything we've been through, do you not know who I am?"

"I didn't… I mean… It was just a kiss. A kiss between friends." Unable to bear his look of disappointment and anger, she looked away. She *had* known better. She *did* know better.

As the waitress delivered their meals, she looked back at him. His hazel eyes no longer danced with the laughter they'd shared earlier in the day. Instead they stared back with a hardness she had never seen before. This was her fault. She had messed up. It had been a good day, a great day, with the both of them easily falling back into the comfort of their longtime friendship. And now she'd let her jealousy ruin it. Jealousy to which she had no right. Jealousy that she could never admit to him without revealing the feelings she still had for him. Feelings that could ruin the friendship they were working so hard to mend.

And she wouldn't do that. Scott's friendship was too important. She couldn't let her old teenage desire for more destroy this one last chance they had to make things right between the two of them. She needed his friendship too much. Over the last few weeks, she had come to realize just how much she needed him.

Scott tried to fight back his anger as he walked Felicity to her door. He had tried to let it go, he really had, but just thinking about her questioning him about another woman made him even angrier. How could someone who had known him so well think that he would kiss her if he had someone he was involved with back at home? It didn't make sense.

Had their time apart changed him so much that she didn't recognize him for the man he was? He didn't think so. She knew him, *really* knew him. She had no reason for asking him something that questioned the very principles he lived by of being honest and upfront with everyone.

And then there was that comment she had made about it just being a kiss between friends. There had been nothing friendly about the kiss, as far as he was concerned. Maybe it hadn't been as passionate as some of the kisses they'd shared before, but it had meant more to him than what she seemed willing to accept.

And that just made his blood boil. She seemed so sure that all there was left between them was friendship, when he knew there could be more.

"Do you want to come in?" she asked as she unlocked her door.

Walking inside with her right now would be a mistake. He was too wound up in emotions that could explode at any minute. So what, he was going to just keep all this inside? No. He'd show her just how honest and up-front he could be.

He took a step inside and could immediately tell that she'd hoped he wouldn't. As usual, this new Fliss wanted to avoid anything that could complicate her world. Well, tonight he was going to be her complication.

"I'll make some coffee," she said as she moved past him toward the kitchen.

Her body brushed against his, and that was all it took for his body to burst into flames. He caught her wrist with his hand and very gently pulled her close to him. He didn't want to scare her. He would never do that.

"I think we need to set a few things straight." Her body relaxed against his. There was no way she could ignore the proof of his desire as he held her against his hard body. Had she really thought that all the desire he'd felt for her before they'd parted had just died away? Had she thought that because she had decided that she needed to end things between them, all the emotion and desire that he'd felt for her would cease to exist? That he could have just replaced her with someone else that easily?

It was as if, unknowingly, he'd spent half his life waiting for Felicity Dale. For her to grow up. For her to come to London. For her to realize she'd made a mistake when she'd sent him away. He was tired of waiting.

"What are we doing, Scott?" Her voice was husky with a sound he'd only heard once before. The memories of the night they'd shared in his bed made him rock-hard.

"I think it's time we quit avoiding the elephant in the room. We slept together, Fliss. And we both enjoyed it. A lot. That attraction, that desire, it's still there whether you want to accept it or not. That's a fact. Now it's up to you to decide what you want to do about it. I know what I want. You know what I want. It's up to you if we take this any further, but while you're thinking about it, you need to think about this too." He lowered his head to hers and waited for her to pull back. Instead she moved toward him, her lips already parting for his when they met. The taste of her filled his mouth, and he immediately remembered all the other parts of her he'd tasted that one night they'd pleasured each other.

His body went hot with a need he hadn't known since the last time he'd held her. He ran one hand through her silky hair and pulled her closer with the other that remained around her waist. He wouldn't do more. Not tonight. He wouldn't take what he needed from her just because of the heat of the moment. She needed to accept that there was still something between them before they could move any further.

Her moan was the sweetest sound he'd ever heard. Yeah, she still wanted him. He softened his hold on her and stepped back as he raised his head. Her lips were wet from his kisses, her blond silky strands tangled in his fingers. Her eyelids slowly opened, revealing soft blue eyes heavy with what he knew was desire for him.

It hurt from his groin to his heart to step away from her, but he knew it was the right thing to do. Fliss had never been one to make spontaneous decisions.

And after the way she'd sent him away before, he needed to know that she wanted, *needed*, him as much as he needed her. It was Fliss's decision if they went any further. He'd left New York feeling unwanted and unneeded. It had been a blow not only to his pride but also to his heart. He didn't want to leave here feeling that way a second time.

He took another step away, then walked back out the door. He'd wait for her. He just hoped she didn't make him wait too long. Their time was quickly running out.

CHAPTER NINE

"IT'S MISSING SOMETHING," Dr. Mason said as he looked around the new cardiac center.

Felicity scanned the area. There was nothing missing. The new center was beautiful with everything so shiny and new. The light gray walls perfectly complemented the faux-wood floors with their gray tint. The chrome-and-glass light fixtures worked well with all the state-of-the-art monitors displayed at the modern glass nurses' station. Even the signage on the walls had been designed to be practical but also decorative. There was absolutely nothing missing.

"The contractors have assured us that all the paint touch-ups will be done by the end of the day and the bio-med team will have the display monitors up and running by this afternoon," Scott said, then turned back to her. "Is there anything you're aware of that hasn't been completed?"

"No. The stocking of supplies is complete and you can see that all the furniture has been placed properly," she said. It had been a fight to get the furniture here on time, but it was done.

"No, that's not what I meant. The unit is beautiful. It's everything I and the board hoped for. It's just…" Dr. Mason looked back around the unit.

Scott looked over at her and shrugged his shoulders. She had checked everything off her lists. It was all complete.

"It just needs a bit of Christmas, I think," Dr. Mason said. "That's it. That's what it's missing."

"But, Dr. Mason, it's a beautiful unit. It's perfect just the way it is now." She'd fight the man before someone hung a fake garland or a bunch of giant red balls on her brand-new unit.

"The rest of the hospital's been decorated for weeks now. We can't open up here without a little bit of Christmas cheer." Dr. Mason turned in place as he took in the whole panorama of the unit before stopping in front of Scott and Felicity. "You've both done a great job here. And I know the important thing is going to be the great difference we're going to make to the community once we open. But impressions are important, and I know we're going to make a great one on Monday when we do our first tour. It just needs a touch of the season to warm it up. Nothing flashy, just a touch. I trust you two to know what it needs."

They waited until Dr. Mason had left the unit before looking at each other.

"Okay, Father Christmas. What's your plan? Because I can tell you right now, we are not going to clutter this place up with some gaudy decorations, no matter what he wants." They'd worked too hard to let their grand opening be ruined by Dr. Mason's need for some Christmas cheer.

"I agree, but we can't just ignore his request," Scott said as he walked over to the nurses' station.

"And it's a little late to try to find decorations from the warehouse. Everything's already been taken by the other departments." She watched as Scott walked back to the automatic doors that opened into the unit, then turned and studied the nurses' station again. She was glad he was at least busy concentrating on something besides her. She'd caught him watching her several times over the last week and it had been unnerving. She had started to remind him that they needed to concentrate on the job, but that would have meant having a personal conversation, and she wasn't ready for that. Right now she preferred for all their concentration to be on the new unit. It was safer that way.

Not that all her own concentration had been on the job. She'd spent several nights that week wide-awake, unable to keep her mind from playing over the kiss that had almost had her begging Scott to take her to bed. She was working sixteen-hour days, but the moment her head hit her pillow, all she thought about was the way Scott had felt pressed against her. So hard. So ready to take their friendship to another level, somewhere they had been only once before. But was that what she wanted?

Yes, she wanted it. Physically, she knew they were good together. But where did they go from there?

And that was the problem. She never could just accept the here and now. She always worried about the future. She always had to know what the plan was going forward. Maybe that was part of the reason she'd sent Scott away. There'd been no plan. They'd taken their friendship to a place where it could be changed forever. And it had done just that. But that had been her choice. Just like Scott had left it up to her whether they took things any further now.

"I think we can do it," Scott said, startling her.

"Do what?" Her head whipped around to where he was standing. Had he read her mind?

That was one of the scary parts of their relationship: he knew her too well.

"All we really need is a little something as you first enter the unit. Just a touch of decoration that warms the place up—just a little bit of sparkle," he said, studying the area he had chosen in which to make a statement.

"A touch of sparkle? Like the crystal snowflake ornaments you got for my tree?" she asked. She could see it now. "Blue lights—pale blue like the ones on my tree. We could string some around the outside of the nurses' station here, then a small tree over here."

She walked behind the front desk and cleared a spot where a small basket had been stored for keeping discharged patient files. She still felt the unit was fine as it was, but if they had to decorate, at least this way it wouldn't detract from its clean, modern look. "If we can't find a tree or the ornaments, I can donate my tree."

"It will have to be an artificial one to pass the fire code. There were still some small artificial ones at the hobby shop where I picked up your ornaments. I'll run over there now. Do you want to go?" Scott asked.

"I can't. I still have an appointment," she said. He sent her a look that said he didn't believe her. "I have a late interview for that last open RN position."

"Good. You can help me when I get back, then." He smiled at her for the first time in days. "Dr. Mason was right. With just a few decorations, it will be perfect."

"It's perfect now," she grumbled as he left the unit. But she had to admit, she was looking forward to seeing how it would look once they added just a little bit of Christmas.

The interview went well, and by the time Scott returned she had made the job offer and emailed all the paperwork to the human resources department.

"Did you buy out the store?" she asked as she took one of the bags from him.

"Just the lights—the blue ones, that is. We need a lot more to go around the nurses' station than we did for your tree." He set the rest of the bags and boxes down on the counter.

"If you want to start on the lights, I've got some of those hooks with the suction cups that won't leave a mark."

By the time he returned with a small tree, she had all of the lights pulled out of their boxes and strung together. They worked as a team and quickly had the lights hung and the tree decorated. When they both stepped back, she was happy to see that Scott had been right. The decorations were perfect.

"It's perfect. Look at it. The whole place looks perfect," Felicity said as Scott plugged in the lights. "Though I still think it looked fine before."

"It did look fine, just a bit empty," Scott said as he came around to stand by her.

"What it needs is patients and staff. I can't wait till this opening is over so we can finally make use of the space. One of the emergency-room nurses I talked to yesterday said the wait time to be seen yesterday was up to four hours. Can you imagine sitting in the waiting room that long?" She started to walk through the unit, turning off lights as she went.

"Just be prepared for there to be some problems. When we first opened our unit in London there was a real learning curve concerning which patients to send to the ER and which need to come straight to the cardiac center," Scott said as he followed her.

"I know, but my staff is up for the challenge." She noticed just how quiet the unit was as they walked back to their office to lock up. This evening had been the first time they'd been alone since he'd left her apartment the day they'd been shopping together. She'd expected it to be awkward for the two of them to work together, like it had been when he'd first arrived. Instead Scott had treated her as if nothing had happened between the two of them. As if he'd never kissed her, then walked out, leaving her to decide where their relationship went from there. And where could it really go? He would be leaving in less than three weeks. Of course, they could become lovers until then.

"About the other night…" she started, then stopped. Was this really the time and place to start this conversation?

"Yes?" Scott said. Of course, he wasn't going to make this easy for her.

"I just wanted you to know…" Know what? That she had visions of jumping his body every time she shut her eyes to go to sleep? Why was everything so difficult between them now? Why couldn't she just tell him how much his kisses had affected her? How much she wanted him to kiss her again?

"Look, Fliss, I wasn't trying to pressure you into something you don't want. I just felt like you needed to know where I was coming from. I want you, and I think you want me. But I've been wrong about us before."

His reminder that she had ended things between them stung, though she couldn't fault him for it. He had never understood why she'd wanted to end things between them, even though he had understood that she couldn't leave her parents. He'd never understand how hard that had been for her or why she had thought it would be best for him if the two of them had a clean break.

"It's late and we've got a big day tomorrow. We can talk about this later," he said. He turned the last of the lights out behind them as they walked out.

As they left the hospital and went their separate ways, her excitement for the grand opening the next day was forgotten. All she could concentrate on was where things stood between her and Scott. She was torn in two different directions. One part of her wanted to do what she knew the old Felicity would do: decide what she wanted and go for it. But the other part of her, the one she had become over the last year and a half, that Felicity wanted to do the responsible and safe thing.

No matter what decision she made, there was one thing neither one of them could forget. Scott would be leaving the day after New Year's Day. Their time together was running out. He had left it up to her what happened between them. Was she brave enough to make a decision that could cause them to lose everything they had rebuilt in the last few weeks?

And if she let this chance with Scott go?

You will regret it for the rest of your life.

It was strange sitting at the new nurses' station with the rest of the staff, waiting for a sick patient to arrive. Usually they'd all be enjoying a break in the action, but not today. Scott stretched his legs out in front of him and adjusted his seat. He'd never been one for waiting for something to happen.

The grand opening that day had gone by fast, with the morning dedicated to giving tours of the unit, first to the hospital board members and then to other staff members, until after noon, when the department officially opened for business.

The phone rang and Felicity quickly answered it. "Brooklyn Heights Cardiac Center."

Scott waited as she took down some notes. "Bring him over. We're ready."

"Fifty-five-year-old male. Shortness of

breath. Chest pain radiating down his left arm for thirty minutes. ETA by ground ambulance, ten minutes," she said as she stood and, with the charge nurse, headed to the triage room they had decided would be used for their first patient.

Minutes later two paramedics came in with the expected patient. After helping them move the patient over to the exam table, everyone began to work on the man at once.

"Hi, I'm Dr. Thomas. How are you feeling right now?"

"Not good. This pain is bad. Real bad." The man's voice quivered as he spoke.

"We're going to give you something to help with that right now." Scott nodded to one of the nurses as she drew up the morphine.

"Do you see a cardiologist—" Scott looked down at the paperwork the EMS crew had left "—Mr. Lawrence?"

"Yeah, I had a couple stents put in about a year ago," the man said.

Scott leaned over the patient and began to do his assessment. His skin was damp and his color had become cyanotic. It was clear he was in distress.

One of the nurses who had been left to man the desk stuck her head into the room. "The ER just called. There's a woman in triage with atypical chest pain with EKG changes. They're on their way now. I'm putting them in room three."

"I'll be right there," Felicity said as she started to pull off her gloves.

"You stay here. I'll take this one," said Anna, the charge nurse, as she left the room.

"Is someone getting a twelve-lead?" Scott called out as he studied the rhythm on the monitor on the wall. It clearly showed he was having an MI.

"I've got it," one of the nurses said as she ripped it off the machine and handed it to him.

"Fliss, call the cath lab. I need him there now," Scott said. The EKG clearly showed ST elevations. "We'll use the new room. I just need a team," Scott said as Felicity picked up the phone and punched in numbers. With the cath lab and new center working side by side, this man had a better chance of survival.

"He's gone unresponsive," one of the nurses called. "Blood pressure falling along with heart rate."

Scott quickly checked for a femoral pulse. It was weak but it was there. He noted how cool the patient's skin was against his hand.

"He's going into cardiogenic shock," Scott said as he began pulling the monitors off the man. "We need to go now."

"Have the cath team set up for a balloon pump," he said to Felicity.

"Already done," she said. She joined him and the rest of the staff as they rushed the man's stretcher toward the back entrance to the interventional lab.

"Good luck," Felicity said as she left him.

He looked down at his watch. It had been less than ten minutes since the patient had arrived in the new unit. It looked like luck was already on his side.

An hour later, when Scott had returned to the unit, almost every room had been filled.

Joining Felicity at the front desk, he looked over the central monitors, where he could observe the vital signs and cardiac rhythms from all the patient rooms.

"Welcome to our grand opening," Felicity said with a smile.

"Looks a bit different from this morning, doesn't it?" Scott said as he took a seat.

"Apparently rumors are already circling. Dr. Mason has been back down here and he was very happy when I told him about our success with our first patient," she said.

"The patient has a long way to go, but at least we gave him a good chance. The fact that he made it to the cath lab so fast is definitely a point in his favor." There was no doubt in Scott's mind that if the patient had been kept waiting in the emergency room, he wouldn't have made it.

"Anyone I need to see first?" he asked.

"We called the on-call cardiologist for orders on the woman in room three that came in after Mr. Lawrence and started serial cardiac enzymes on her. She's stable." She pulled up the strip so he could review it. "There's an older man in room five that you should probably see next. He stopped his diuretic and is in new onset atrial fibrillation."

"Okay, that's my next stop, then. If there are any issues, just text me," he said as he headed back down the hallway.

He'd always enjoyed this part of the job. Working shoulder to shoulder with the nurses and giving direct care to his patients was more satisfying than any other part of his job. The fact that he was getting to share this with Felicity made the experience even more enjoyable, as they'd always been so compatible at work. It was like she knew what he was thinking before he did, which was a bit disturbing considering some of the things he had been thinking lately when he had been around her.

But there was nothing he could do about that. There was more than just mere attraction between the two of them. There always had been. But how long was it going to take for her to accept that? He just hoped she didn't wait too long. The opening of the unit and his work here was almost complete. In less than three weeks, he would be on his way back to London, and this chance to find out what was left between them would be gone.

Felicity had worked many long shifts on cardiac units and later in the emergency room, and none of them had been more demanding than the last twelve hours. Now she sat back at her desk and stared at the computer screen that showed her the day's payroll information, which she needed to approve by the next morning. Finally, when it began to look like the little squiggly lines were chasing each other across the screen, she knew she had to take a break. Closing her eyes, she rested her head on her desk for just a moment.

Too many restless nights caused by memories of that night they'd shared in London were catching up with her and it was all Scott's fault. If he hadn't kissed her that last time in her apartment, those memories would have been left buried. Instead, each night she closed her eyes, she was reminded of every touch, every kiss, that they had shared.

She had planned the rest of their lives around that one night. Their engagement would take place on a romantic trip some-place in the English countryside and their wedding would be an event that their home-town would talk about for days. She'd even planned the children she knew they would have in the years to come: a boy and a girl with their father's dark hair and her blue eyes. It had just been silly musings as Scott had lain next to her. But there had been such a happiness in her heart that night, which had given her hope that finally the two of them would have a future together.

Who could have known that in a few hours both of their lives would change in such a horrible way?

But she wasn't going to let herself think about that right now. She just needed to rest her eyes. Just for a minute.

"Fliss, wake up," Scott said from some-where beside her.

"No, go away." She turned her head away from the voice that was disturbing her dreams. She wanted to go back to that deep, soft bed where a warm and naked Scott lay next to her. "So nice."

"Fliss, honey, you can't sleep here tonight."

She felt a warm hand run up and down her arm. Opening her eyes, she met soft hazel ones only inches from hers. She recognized those eyes. She leaned over and kissed their owner. "Hey."

She lifted her head up so she could see him better, then noticed his green scrub top. "You've got clothes on."

His strangled cough and laugh stirred something awake in her mind. She made herself lift her head and look around the room. This wasn't Scott's apartment in London.

She groaned and tucked her head between her arms. She'd fallen asleep and had been dreaming. Maybe if she stayed this way, he'd leave her to die of embarrassment alone.

"Do you want to talk about it?" Scott asked.

He'd moved away from her, but she could still hear the amusement in his voice.

"No. I want to go back to sleep." She refused to look up. Eventually he would have to leave. She'd just have to outwait him.

"So you can go back to sleep and dream of me without my clothes on?" he asked, his mouth now close to her ear.

She jumped up, connecting with his face.

"Ouch," he said as he put his hand to his jaw, then gave her a wicked smile. "You awake now?"

"Yes, I'm awake, thank you." She moved away from him as she talked. This sexy, flirty Scott was dangerous. "And now I'm going to go home."

She grabbed her computer and started stuffing it into her bag. She'd finish whatever it was that she'd been working on when she got home. Right now her priority was to get away from Scott.

She'd kissed the man and revealed that she'd been dreaming of him without his clothes on, all while being alone in her office. Her work office. And now he was grinning at her like the big bad wolf who wanted to take a bite out of Red Riding Hood.

She just didn't have words. There were none that could undo this embarrassment. She started toward the door.

"You might want to take your coat. It can be cold out there if you don't have enough clothes on."

She went back to the hook beside the door and grabbed her coat before slamming the door behind her. She heard the laughter coming from behind the door and groaned.

She had made it out of the hospital and half-way down the block to the subway before she slowed her steps. The man was never going to let her live this one down and she couldn't blame him. It wasn't something she would likely forget herself. She'd embarrassed herself many times before in her life, but this would be one for the records.

There was no way she could hide the fact that she wanted to be in Scott's bed now. It was so tempting to just come out and tell him that she wanted to sleep with him. She'd all but told him so tonight. He'd made it clear it was up to her to decide where they took their relationship next. And just because she wanted to become sexually involved with him again didn't mean that there would be any talk of a future. Scott knew her reasons for staying in the States just like she understood that his place was in London at the job he had worked so hard for.

They were two adults who were attracted to each other physically. There was no reason that they couldn't enjoy each other's company physically. Wasn't that just what they had been doing while she was in London? She might have had big dreams about a future after they'd slept together, but neither of them had made any mention of such a future. There had been no talk of love.

Maybe all Scott wanted was a physical relationship. That was okay. She could agree to that. Couldn't she?

All she had to do was go into things with an acceptance that this was just a temporary relationship between the two of them. Maybe this was what she needed in order to move on with her life. To move past her crush on Scott.

Now all she had to do was find some way to tell Scott that she wanted him without making an even bigger fool of herself than she had already.

CHAPTER TEN

SATURDAY MORNING, FELICITY was shocked to find herself out shopping with the rest of the holiday-weary crowd on the last weekend before Christmas. She had always prided herself on getting her shopping done long before the desperate shoppers hit the stores. But here she was, seven days before Christmas, with eyes glazed over from too much window-shopping and feet that would be sporting blisters the next day.

The opening week in the new cardiac department had been a huge success. There had been some issues, mainly on the physicians' side, with policies that needed to be addressed—such as which patients would be escalated to the cardiac center after originally being seen in the emergency room—but Scott had been there to handle those while she had concentrated more on her staff and their patients. And to ensure she didn't find herself being caught asleep at her desk again, she'd started bringing all her administrative work home with her. Not that it mattered—they'd both been too tied up to do more than greet each other in the morning and say good-night as the next shift came in to relieve them.

She'd therefore not had a chance to approach Scott with her decision to take their relationship further—at least, that was what she was telling herself.

She'd stopped to admire the display of assorted Christmas trees made up from colorful men's ties in bold solids and multicolored stripes. Looking at the store's name on the sign above the door, she realized that this was the small department store she had visited all those years ago as a teenager, shopping for a special present for Scott. The one where she had discovered the scent that she now associated with him.

Had she stopped and admired the store's window display that year? She couldn't remember. Staring at the window, she caught her own reflection. She'd changed so much since then. There were physical changes, of course. Those irritating braces that had plagued her teenage years had been replaced by the straight white teeth the orthodontist had promised and she'd finally moved out of the training-bra section when she'd made it to her sophomore year in high school.

But there was more than that. She'd been a shy teenager, which was one of the reasons she'd followed her brother and his friends around so much, always hanging in the background, never wanting to bring too much attention to herself. Now she stood a little straighter and she was a lot bolder than she'd been before. She had become more confident, something she owed to Scott's encouragement, when she had become a nurse. And she'd been willing to work hard for what she wanted, which had paid off when she had applied for her new position. So why couldn't she make herself move on with her personal life?

Because she was afraid. She'd built up her idea of what her perfect life was going to be, and when she'd lost Leo, she'd lost that perfect dream. She was a nurse. She knew life was messy and difficult and sometimes ended in heartbreaking ways, but for some reason she hadn't ever thought that would be her life. But now she knew that, like every other human, she had no guarantee. And without that guarantee she was too afraid to take the next step.

She turned to face one of the mirrors on the shop wall and looked herself in the eye. It was time for her to move on, and the first thing she needed to do was grab this opportunity to be with Scott for the short time they had together. She looked over to where the ties dangled from a tall, thin tree. To start, she would find the perfect present to show him that she did still care for him.

As the store doors opened and she entered, she felt a little bit more Christmas spirit awaken inside her. This might be the only Christmas they would ever get to spend together. It wouldn't be perfect, not without her brother here, but she was going to make great memories that she could relive for the years that were to come. And for now that would just have to be enough.

Felicity waited till the end of the day to approach Scott with her invitation. He'd spent most of the day on the unit, only having to take one patient over to the cath lab for an intervention, but she'd never found quite the right opportunity, and with the next day being Christmas Eve, time was running out.

"About Christmas," she started, as he stepped into their office.

"We're not back to that again, are we? There's no reason for you to take a train when I'm already making the trip in the car." Scott's voice held a note of agitation she wasn't used to hearing, but they were both tired, so she let it go.

"No. It's not that. I was thinking..." she caught herself looking down at her shoes and made herself look up "...maybe you'd like to come over the night before and we could just leave from my place the next morning."

She knew the moment he realized she was inviting him to spend the night with her when his eyes shot to hers and didn't leave.

"Are you sure?" he asked as he walked toward her.

He stopped in front of her with only inches between them. Desire sparked between them with an energy that shocked her heart into a dangerous rhythm.

"Oh, yeah. I'm very sure." Her voice was thick with a passion she'd denied for too long. She wanted this man, no matter what the outcome might be. If only she had admitted this to herself earlier. She'd wasted so much time fighting it.

He pushed a small strand of hair that had come loose from its tie behind her ear and let his finger linger as it traced a path from her ear down her neck. Was he remembering how sensitive her neck was to the touch of his lips? How she'd cried out for him when he'd bitten that perfect spot between her neck and collarbone as she came? Did he remember every touch, every kiss, the way she did?

Her breath caught in her throat and she stepped closer.

"Not here. Not like this," he said as he brushed another unseen hair back from her face, then stepped away. "Tomorrow. We'll have the whole night."

She took a deep breath and calmed her breathing. He was right. This wasn't the place.

"I'm only scheduled for half the day tomorrow, so I can take care of supper." She moved as far away from him as possible while she gathered her bag and coat.

"I'll make a bargain with you. If you can help me wrap a few presents, I'll bring dinner," Scott said.

"You haven't wrapped a thing, have you?" Felicity couldn't help but laugh at his guilty look. His mother had always spoiled him by wrapping his presents for him.

"I had most of them wrapped at the store. It's just the ones when we went shopping together at the market that need to be wrapped."

"Okay, dinner is on you," she said as she opened the door to leave.

"And after dinner?" he asked.

"That's all on you too," she said before shutting the door. She'd done it. She'd made a decision that would move things forward with Scott. And if the last few minutes were any sign, there would be no waiting till after dinner.

Scott knocked on Felicity's door and waited. It felt like he had done a lot of waiting for Felicity. And after her reaction to him the night before in the office, waiting for tonight had been especially difficult. Everywhere he had turned that day, he'd seen her, and his mind happily sent him memories of the two of them together that one night in his apartment in London.

He repositioned the box he held in his arm, then switched the takeout bag and his duffel bag into his other hand so he could check his jacket pocket. He felt the length of the small jewelry box and relaxed. Of all the Christmas gifts he had bought, this one was the most important to him.

The door opened and he fumbled the box in his arm. Dressed in a red formfitting dress that skimmed the tops of her knees and matching high heels that had his mouth watering, Felicity was a sight even his imagination had been unable to dream up. Gone were the boxy hospital scrubs and the comfy jeans that he associated with his friend Fliss. Instead some beautiful blonde heartbreaker stood in her place. He could do nothing but stand there and stare.

"Here, let me take some of those," she said as she moved toward him.

He cleared his throat, then entered the apartment while making sure that he kept some space between the two of them. "No, I've got them."

Scott looked around the room. There had been some changes here too. A poinsettia sat on the table along with two red candles and a small nativity scene on the fireplace mantel. Pillows in soft blues lay on the couch with a throw blanket that matched. The apartment had seemed so sterile and unwelcoming the first time he'd seen it, and he'd been shocked at how different it had looked compared to the homey little place she had rented in London. But now, with the small changes she had made, he could see her living here.

"The place looks nice," he said as he crossed the room and placed the rest of the items by the couch.

"Thanks. Someone told me Christmas was coming, so I decided I'd better get ready." She smiled at him as her eyes danced with merriment and his heart turned over. This was the woman he'd been waiting for, the Felicity Dale who was a little bit cheeky and a whole lot of excitement. Somehow she'd found her way back to him and he wasn't willing to wait another minute.

"How hungry are you?" he asked as he slowly made his way over to her.

He came to a stop with barely an inch between them and she didn't move away. Instead she stepped closer, laying her hand on his chest. Did she feel his heart as it hammered in his chest? Did she realize that it beat just for her?

He wrapped his hand around her neck and pulled her closer as he angled his mouth over hers. She opened at the first touch of his lips and he filled his mouth with the sweet taste of her. He wrapped his other arm around her waist and pulled her against him so she could feel the hard length of him. It might be too soon to let her know how much he cared for her, but he wanted her to feel just how much he wanted her. She rubbed her body against his and her moan was more than he could take.

Remembering all those sappy romantic movies she used to make him watch with her, he lifted her up in his arms.

"Wrap your legs around me," he said as he adjusted her body against his, then headed for the only door that led from the room. He placed her on the bed, then unwound her legs from around him one by one. He unstrapped one high heel, then ran his hands up her leg,

massaging her calf and trailing his finger-
tips higher up her thigh until he could go
no farther before placing that leg down and
then repeating his movements on her next
leg. When he got to the top of her thigh this
time, he glided his hand over the red panties
she wore. The soft silk was damp from her
desire for him and he lingered there for a moment, stroking her gently when she opened
her legs for him. Her moans became louder
when he pressed the palm of his hand against
her and he followed the path of his hands with
his lips, stopping when he reached the inside
of her thigh.

"Scott." She moaned his name and something broke inside him. He remembered the
way she had called out his name when he'd
entered her for the first time. He'd taste every
inch of her before the night was over, but
right now he just needed to be inside of her.

Pushing her dress up, he trailed his lips
up her chest to her mouth. Their kisses became desperate and demanding. She helped

him pull her dress over her head and her lacy red bra followed. Moving back to the end of the bed, he made quick work of his own clothes and then stood for a moment, taking in the sight of the passionate woman who lay on the bed before him. She was clad only in red silk panties, her sapphire eyes flashing with desire. Her lips, bruised from their kisses, stood out against her pale porcelain skin. He'd never seen a woman more beautiful than Felicity Dale.

He covered her with his body and they both moaned as he entered her. He took a moment to take in the vision she made as her eyes burned into him. He bent his mouth to her ear and whispered, "Never forget this. Never forget the way I feel inside you, the way we fit so perfectly. Promise me that."

"Yes," she moaned as she arched against him. "I'll always remember."

She arched against him again and he sank into her. He wouldn't let her forget him again.

He began to move inside her as she rocked

against him. He fought for control. He wanted this night to last. She cried out his name and he lost the battle. She shattered around him, and time stood still as all breath left his body and he broke into a million pieces inside her.

When he was able to pull himself back together, he rolled over, taking her with him until she rested on top of him. Brushing his hand against her soft hair, he closed his eyes and let himself drift off.

Felicity had watched Scott from afar for so many years, but she'd never seen him like this. His body relaxed and his respirations were deep and even. At that moment he appeared so vulnerable. She rested her head on his chest and listened to the steady drum of his heartbeat, trying to relax her own body. He'd made her promise that she wouldn't forget the way they fit together and how could she? Never had a man made her feel so desired. Never had she ever felt so much desire for another man. There had never been another man for her.

That thought cleared away the rest of the sexual haze that had engulfed her. That was a dangerous path that her mind wanted to take, and she wasn't ready to find out where it would lead. Too many obstacles lay in the way of this being anything but a fling for the two of them. Nothing had changed since she had sent Scott back to London without her. She still wasn't willing to leave her parents alone. London was so far away. That was what she needed to remember.

But she wasn't going to let that ruin the time they had right now. They had only a few days left together and she wasn't going to waste them. Tomorrow they would spend the day with their families, but the next day they would return to the city, where most of their time would be spent at work. There were only a few hours that they could spend alone together, and they needed to make the most of those. After he was gone, she could sit alone and feel sorry for herself. But not now. Right now she needed to live in the present and enjoy every moment they had left together.

She closed her eyes and rested her head against him. For now she was just going to enjoy the warmth of him against her.

When she opened her eyes later, she was greeted with the spicy smell of tomato sauce. Stretching, she climbed out of bed and grabbed the first thing she saw—Scott's long-sleeved shirt—before she headed into the bathroom. After putting herself back together, she rescued her red panties from the bedsheets, then headed for the kitchen, where she found Scott fighting a piece of Christmas wrapping paper as he tried to cover the small sailboat he had bought his father.

"Hey," he said as he started to get up from the table. "Did you come to rescue me?"

"I think it's your father's present that needs rescuing. Let me see if I can find a box for it," she said as she returned to her bedroom.

When she came back with a small box, the sailboat and wrapping had been removed and plates piled high with red sauce and pasta had taken their place. He had lit the candles and turned the lights down. With the Christmas tree lights and the glow from the fireplace, the room had an intimate feel that was just the mood she had wanted to set earlier in the evening.

"Ready to eat?" he asked as he poured them each a glass of a Moscato wine—her favorite. Still shirtless because she had refused to give him back the shirt that she had on, he'd pulled on only his pants and left the top button undone. He looked good enough to eat himself. Her stomach growled, but she wasn't sure it was from her need for food. They'd both starve to death if she didn't get her mind on something else.

"Sure. Then you can do the dishes while I take care of the presents," she said as she looked over at a mess of Christmas wrapping paper that had been pulled out and piled up on her couch.

They talked about everything—their work, of course, and then their parents' plans for the next day, and Scott even talked about his work in London. They talked about everything, except what she was sure was on both of their minds. But what was there really to say? They'd both enjoy this time together and then things would go back to the way they were before Scott had come back to New York.

No, that wasn't true. She'd changed in the last few weeks. She'd taken a step toward returning to a life that held more for her than just work, and she didn't think she could go back there again.

As she finished wrapping Scott's presents, she glanced over at the opening to her kitchen, where she could see him washing her dishes. He was the proof that there was nothing as sexy as a man doing dishes. Was it wrong to wish for more dirty dishes just so she could continue to watch him? No, not at all.

Making a decision, she pushed the wrapping paper aside and stood. There was only one present left to wrap and it could wait until the morning. The clock on her mantel showed it was fast approaching midnight and she couldn't think of anything she wanted more than Scott for her Christmas present.

Wrapping her arms around him from behind, she ran her hands up his bare chest. He stopped with his hands still holding a serving dish, his body tensed under her hands. The feel of his muscled back against her breast had her rubbing against him just like one of her mother's old cats. Thinking of those cats, she put her mouth to his earlobe and bit down lightly before licking away the sting and whispering into his ear, "It's almost Christmas and I've finally decided what I want."

"And what would that be?" Scott's voice was as tense as his body.

"All I want from Santa this Christmas, right here, right now, is you," she said, moving back as he turned in her arms and placed his soapy hands under her bottom, pulling her against him.

"I think that's something I can take care of without Santa's help," he said as he bent his head to hers, making all her Christmas wishes come true.

CHAPTER ELEVEN

THEY'D HAD TO rush the next morning to get ready to leave for the Christmas dinner at her parents' house. As she packed her bag for the trip, she tried to keep her mind off the fact that she would have to spend tonight alone. There were so few nights left for them that the thought of spending one apart seemed unbearable.

"It will be fine," Scott said as he took her hand and squeezed it as they sat outside her parents' house. "Your parents know what they're doing. If they thought they couldn't handle Christmas at their house, they would have told my parents."

They had held hands on the journey, but when they had stopped in her parents' drive, she had pulled away.

"And I'll be here too," Scott said as he opened the door to his car and climbed out.

"I know," she said when she joined him on the sidewalk.

After making their way inside the house, she found her dad in the living room, watching a football game. She left Scott with all the men as she went into the crowded kitchen and pushed her way past aunts and cousins.

"There you are," her mother said as she pulled Felicity to her for a hug. She let herself relax against her mom's shoulders. Her mom was a strong woman, but Leo's death had shaken her. There was no way for them to get through this holiday get-together without being reminded of her brother.

Felicity pulled away and looked her mom in the eyes. "Are you okay?"

Her mom gave her a watery smile. "It helps that everyone is here."

"You sure?" she asked.

Her mother nodded, then hugged her again. "You smell nice. Kind of woodsy. New perfume?"

"I wondered when you were going to show up," Scott's mother said as she came up behind her.

She'd known that kiss she'd shared with Scott right before they'd arrived had been a mistake.

"Yeah, it's different, right?" Felicity said to her mother before she turned to Scott's.

"Scott's in the den with the rest of the freeloaders waiting for food to magically appear," Felicity said as she tried to move away from the two of them. She had no doubt Scott's mother would recognize her son's scent. Of course, she could use the excuse that she had been closed up in his car on their drive there.

Her mom nodded before she was pulled away to handle someone's question concerning something that had just come out of the oven. Unfortunately Scott's mother remained.

"Your mom is doing fine," she said as they both stared after Felicity's mother. "She's strong. So is your dad. You don't have to worry about them."

"I don't... Okay, I do," Felicity admitted.

"It's just so hard, especially around the holidays. I can't help but worry."

"I know, but you need to understand that they worry about you too. You're their little girl, no matter how old you are," Scott's mother said. "And I'll always be there for your mom. Just like Scott will always be there for you."

Did his mother suspect what was going on between Felicity and Scott? The woman was as intuitive as her son. Did things like that run in families?

"We're actually looking into taking a couples' cruise together for Valentine's," she said, shocking Felicity even more.

Her parents on a cruise? Wouldn't they have a ball, especially with their best friends along with them.

But what if they got sick? They could end up in some primitive hospital that wouldn't be able to take proper care of them. There was that special travel insurance that they could get that would fly them back to the US with a medical flight team.

She realized Scott's mother was waiting on her to say something. Did Scott's mother think she was going to try to talk her parents out of a trip that they deserved? Okay, maybe it had crossed her mind.

"They'll love that," Felicity said as she laid her hand on the other woman's arm and squeezed. "Thank you for being there for Mom and Dad. It means a lot to me to know that you're here for them. I'm still a couple hours away. We're all so lucky to have you close by."

Afraid that her mother would catch sight of her sentimental tears, Felicity excused herself and took the back stairs out of the kitchen and up to the second floor. She stopped at her brother's door. Her parents were going to be okay. They'd survived the last year and they were starting to put their lives back together. Was she holding them back?

"Hi. Mom said I'd find you up here," Scott said as he came up behind her and put an arm across her back. To someone else, they would just look like two friends comforting one another, but she knew the difference now. She leaned into him and rested her head on his shoulder.

"Do the two of you have some type of special power?" she asked, then realized how crazy that sounded. "Don't answer that. It was a stupid question."

"My mom, no. But if you let me in your window tonight, I can show you all my special powers." He wiggled his eyebrows at her and she laughed.

"There's no way you're spending the night with me in my room with my parents downstairs, no matter what your special powers might be," Felicity said as she moved away from him.

He pulled her back into his arms and kissed her with just enough heat to make her consider pulling him into her room right then. "What if I use my special power of being super quiet?"

"Not even an invisibility power is going to get you in there tonight," Felicity said as she took a deep breath and tried to calm her heart.

"We could go down to the lake," Scott said as she started to move away from him.

"And get caught like a bunch of teenagers? In our hometown, where everyone knows us? It would not only embarrass our parents, but it would shock the granny panties off Ms. Connors." She moved farther out of the reach of his arms.

"Why did you have to say that?" he said as he headed for the stairs. "The woman's downstairs and you have to bring up her underwear?"

She followed him down the stairs as he grumbled some more about her ruining Christmas with images of his old schoolteacher that he didn't want to see. Laughing, they joined everyone else who was already gathered around the table, waiting for her father to lead the blessing of the meal. Then chaos broke out in the room as everyone began to pass the food. Scott slipped his hand into hers under the table, and if anyone noticed that Scott seemed to suddenly be eating with his left hand, no one commented.

The merry crowd moved into the living room, where her parents' tree was surrounded by presents, which were quickly given out, and the crowd was dispersed to different areas to start cleaning.

"I love this cookbook," Scott's mother said as she leafed through the yellowed pages. It had been a lucky find in one of the vintage bookstores in the city. "My mother had one just like it, but my sister laid claim to it when we were taking care of my mother's estate. And, Scott, the sweater you bought me is so soft. I've never had real cashmere. And I love this pastel blue color. It's so unlike your usual presents."

"I told you," she said after Scott's mother moved off to thank someone else for their gift.

"And I didn't argue. I'm really not good at buying gifts. Except for yours. I think I did very well with yours," Scott said as he moved in closer and bent down to whisper in her ear. "And I can't wait till I can give it to you."

She and Scott had decided to wait till that evening when they could find somewhere to be alone to exchange their gifts for each other.

Leaving him talking with one of her cousins about the stock market, she went looking for her father, who had bought her a soft brandy-colored leather tote that she could use for work. When she couldn't find him in the living room, she returned to the dining room and found him sitting in a dining-room chair, rubbing his chest.

"Daddy, are you okay?" She rushed to him as she called out for Scott.

"I'm fine, baby girl. It's just a bit of indigestion," he said, though he continued to rub at his chest.

"What is it?" Scott asked, bending down beside Felicity as she took her father's pulse. She counted out the beats as she looked at her watch. His pulse was at a regular rate and rhythm; his skin was dry and his color was good.

"He's having chest pain," she said as she counted her father's respirations. "I need my stethoscope. I think we should call 911," she said as she turned toward Scott.

"Hold on a moment, Fliss. It's not my heart," her father said as he began to stand, only to find her pushing him back down into the chair. "Look, calm down. I just ate too much today. Go get your mother and tell her I need my medicine."

"You're taking medicine? What kind of medicine?" As far as she knew, her father didn't have any health issues.

"I'll go find your mother. I'll be right back," Scott said as he started out of the room, pushing past a crowd that had gathered at the door to the dining room. Felicity hadn't noticed. "Everything's fine now. He just needs to sit for a few minutes."

Her father was a quiet and proud man, and she knew he wouldn't want this kind of attention. This was her fault. She had panicked and now she had made things worse for him.

"I'm sorry, Daddy. I didn't mean to cause a scene." She leaned her head against her father's shoulder.

"It's okay. I should have told you I've been having some stomach issues." Her father looked uncomfortable, but more from embarrassment than pain. "I've got this hiatal hernia and the doctor thinks I need to have a surgical procedure. He's going to do one of those laparoscopic procedures next month."

"Why didn't you tell me?" she asked, though she already knew the answer.

"You worry too much, baby girl. And you've got that new job you're so excited about. We were going to tell you when the time came." Her father looked up as her mother came into the room, carrying a bottle and a glass of water.

"I told you not to overdo it today," her mother said as she handed him the pills and water. "He's supposed to eat smaller meals, you know. But it's Christmas and I didn't want to scold him."

Her father rolled his eyes behind her mother, making Felicity smile.

"It wasn't him. I'm the one that panicked, though I'm glad he told me about the surgical procedure." She turned her eyes back to her mother. "Is there anything else you haven't told me?"

"Of course not, honey. The doctor assured us he would be fine. It's a common enough procedure," her mother said as she patted her husband's hand. "To be honest, it's worrying about upsetting you that's given us the most trouble."

Felicity stared at her mother and father. Had she been hovering so much that now they felt the need to tiptoe around their problems so she didn't become upset? "I'm sorry. I don't mean to worry. And I certainly don't mean to worry the two of you."

"We know that," her father said. "We just want you to live your life and be happy."

She moved away from him. Why did everyone think she wasn't happy?

"While your father's medication starts working, why don't you go with me to run Ms. Connors home?" Scott asked from beside her. "If that's okay with your parents?"

"Of course it's okay. We appreciate you running Irma home," Felicity's mother said. "I'll sit here with your daddy, Fliss. You go with Scott."

Scott took her hand and pulled her up. "She's waiting at the door for us."

Felicity grabbed her coat and helped the older woman down the steps to the sidewalk. She let Scott take charge of the conversation as he drove. She didn't want to talk. She wanted to think.

"I never intended to make things worse for my parents," she said when Scott returned from helping Ms. Connors into her house.

"You didn't make things worse, Fliss. They just worry about you, like all parents worry. My mother worries that I'm going to grow old all alone. My father worries that I'm not preparing for my retirement. Different worries, I know, but they can really get wound up about it." Scott put the car into Reverse, but instead of turning back toward her house, he turned out of the neighborhood and took a road that led into the park. He parked where they could watch some of the kids try out the new sleds they'd just received that morning from Santa, while those more experienced shot past them as they slid down the hill.

"I wanted to give you this here," he said as he handed her a small jeweler's box. He hadn't attempted to wrap it. Instead it had red ribbon that he had tied into a neat bow around it. She recognized the insignia. It was the same one that had been on the jewelry bag that had caused her so much jealousy over another woman who didn't exist.

"I don't have yours with me. It's back at the house in my suitcase," she said as she turned the box over in her hand. "It doesn't seem right opening this without you having yours."

"You can give it to me when we get back to your parents' house. Just open it already.

You know you want to," Scott said. He was watching her with so much pleasure. Whatever was in the box had to mean something special to him.

Sliding the ribbon off, she opened the box and stared at the beautiful white-gold snowflake that was covered in small diamonds, with one larger one in its center, hanging from a delicate white-gold chain.

"It's beautiful."

Suddenly it made sense why he had brought her here to give it to her. He wanted it to be a remembrance of their time together in the snow.

"I love it," she said as she bent over the console of the seat and kissed him. Their lips touched and lingered together for a moment, and then he reached for her. As one hand tangled in her hair, the other cupped her face. Letting go of the small box, she opened her mouth and her hands slipped around his neck, curling into his hair.

A child shouted close beside the car and they broke apart. Looking around, they both laughed when they saw it was only a child calling out for his mother.

"I really like my gift," she said as she settled back against the car seat.

"I'm glad," he said as he relaxed into his own seat.

They watched the kids in the park until the sun started to go down and everyone began to head home. By the time they made it back to Felicity's parents' house, the crowd had gone, along with Scott's parents. After checking on her dad, Scott excused himself so he could spend some time with his own parents before he had to return to the city. It would be the last time he would see them before he returned to London.

It wasn't until she was getting ready for bed that she remembered the present she hadn't given him.

There was a tapping sound coming from his window. Scott turned over and groaned. He'd been tossing for two hours and now this. Had some bird gotten caught up in the screen?

Climbing out of bed, he opened the curtains, but couldn't see a thing in the darkness. Suddenly a bright light blinded him and he stumbled back against a chair. He was about to shout out to his father that there was an intruder when he saw Fliss's face pressed against the window.

"Everything okay, son?" his father called from the room next door.

"Sorry, just got up for…something…and slipped," he said as he put his finger to his lips to warn her not to make a sound. When his father didn't answer him back, he figured it was safe to assume he'd fallen back to sleep.

Scott slid the window up carefully and was greeted by a small wrapped package in a gloved hand that was shivering.

"What are you doing here?" he asked, as he leaned out the window into the cold air. The weather channel had called for temperatures in the twenties, but the windchill meant it felt much colder.

"I wanted you to have your Christmas present before Christmas was over," she said as her teeth chattered.

"Get in here," he said as he reached out for her, but she pulled away.

"I've got to get back before my parents miss me." She leaned in and kissed him with lips as cold as ice. "I hope you like it."

Before he could say another word, she turned and headed off into the dark. He waited for a minute, hoping she'd come back, before finally shutting the window. Picking up the package, he removed the carefully wrapped paper, then opened the small jewelry box. Lying on a white cushion was a tie-pin in the shape of a Christmas tree with a small diamond sitting on its top. Too awake to sleep now, he sat on the bed and stared at the small Christmas tree. It wasn't something he would have chosen for himself, but he knew he would wear it every Christmas for the rest of his life in remembrance of his and Felicity's time together.

Finally he put the box down and climbed back into bed. He knew he'd dream of Fliss tonight. He just didn't know if it would be memories of their time together or fantasies of a future he wasn't sure they would ever have.

CHAPTER TWELVE

SCOTT FOUND FELICITY in the storage closet with a clipboard and a pen. He pulled the door shut behind him.

"Hey," she said as she turned when he came into the small room. "Are you already finished for the day?"

"I am, but I can wait for you," Scott said. He moved behind her, placed his arms around her and nuzzled her neck. "Because you're definitely worth waiting for."

"Scott," she said as she pulled away from him. "My nurses are right down the hall."

"I shut the door," he said, laughing at the shocked look on her face.

"It doesn't have a lock. Anyone could come in." She moved over to another shelf of medical supplies and pretended to ignore him.

The hospital had been busy after Christmas

and it was no surprise to either of them that their time together had been limited to quick conversations in passing at work.

But the nights... They'd made the most of every moment of those. He'd checked out of his hotel the day after Christmas and moved in with Felicity that night so that there would be no wasted time going back and forth. Instead, each night they would rush home and cook together—okay, he did most of the actual cooking—and then they'd fall into bed together, both of them anxious and desperate for that first moment when they would come together, skin to skin. They'd free their passion for each other from the chains they kept in place while pretending to be only coworkers to everyone else around them. Only, it still wasn't enough. There was still something missing when they came together, something that Fliss was holding back from him.

"All right, I'm done," she said as she closed her clipboard and moved toward him. "The rest can wait till tomorrow. Let's go home."

Home. Didn't that sound nice? But where

was his home? His parents had set down roots in the same town and in the same house where they had first married. In some ways that house still felt like home. Not the small bedroom where he'd spent his childhood, but the comfortable atmosphere that told him this was where he belonged. This was where he could be himself. He'd almost achieved that in his own apartment in London. But there always seemed to be something missing.

Except for that one night with Felicity.

That night had made everything in his life feel right. Just like tonight when they'd enter her small apartment and everything would feel right. Like he had come home.

"I received an interesting invitation from Dr. Mason today," Scott said as he started the car. "One of the board members is having this high-class New Year's Eve party tomorrow night and invited us to attend."

"Us?" Felicity said as she turned toward him. "Or you?"

"Where I go, you go," he said, then winced at the words. Not that he didn't wish the words were true, but that would have to be Fliss's choice. He wouldn't demand that she come anywhere with him, no matter what it might cost him.

And he knew that if he pushed her, she'd run—or more likely push him totally out of her life. He'd let her do that before. It wasn't going to happen again. He'd fight for their friendship if that was all they could have together.

And he'd fight for the future he could see for the two of them, but he wouldn't let himself be hurt again. The loss of Leo and then of Felicity had been too much. His first months back in London had been miserable for both him and the people around him. It was only his work that had saved him then. He wasn't prepared to revisit that pain. He had picked himself up and started over once. He wasn't sure he could repeat it.

"The invitation was for two, but I could tell that Dr. Mason was expecting you would be the plus-one." The older man was very astute, something that had surely helped him climb the ladder to the cardiac medical chief position.

"Where's the venue?" she asked, then whistled when he told her the name of the hotel. "That place is amazing. I don't have anything to wear to a place like that."

"You have that red dress. You look amazing in that dress." Just thinking about that outfit was enough to set his body blazing with his need for her. They would definitely be having another late-night dinner. Some things a body needed more than food and sleep.

"Too simple. It needs to be dressier. I'm thinking something classic for a party at a place like that," she said, as she looked out the car window, then turned back to him. "Don't worry. I know the owner of a little vintage store that's bound to have something."

But her smile seemed sadder than he had expected, not excited like he had thought she would be at the opportunity of a night out on the town.

"It's okay if you don't want to go," he said. He parked the car, then turned to her. "It will be fine. I know you're too busy at work to have to worry about getting prepared for a last-minute invitation to a party."

"It's not that. Any other time I'd love to go to a swanky New Year's Eve party." She bit down on her lip before she continued. "But we only have three more nights before you leave. I don't want to share you with all of those other people."

He grabbed her hand and pulled her into the apartment building and up the stairs. "And I don't want to share you with anyone else either. I'll just tell them we have other plans."

"You can't do that. Dr. Mason is expecting you. Maybe we can just stay a little while. If we slip out early, no one will notice," she said as he took her keys and opened her door.

"That will work," he said as he pulled her inside the apartment. "I've just got one question."

As soon as the door shut, she was in his arms. "What's that?"

She had wound her arms around his neck,

and his body was instantly aroused. "What would it take to get you back into that little red dress?"

"Wow," Scott said as she turned in a circle, letting the hem of the long blue sequined dress brush against the floor.

Finding the perfect dress for such an occasion on New Year's Eve day had been a miracle and a hit to her monthly budget, but seeing that look in his eyes made it worth curbing her daily trips to the specialty coffee shop across from the hospital. With the dress's open back and low neckline, along with its fitted waist, it looked as if it had been made for a night on the red carpet. Of course, the fact that she'd found it in a secondhand store meant that it could actually have walked one of those red carpets.

"But it has sequins," Scott said as he joined her in front of the mirror, wearing a classic black suit and snowy white shirt. She knew they would make a stunning entrance tonight.

"You don't like sequins?" she asked as she

made one more attempt to get a good look at the back of the dress. The salesclerk had assured her that the dress covered all the necessary parts, but there seemed to be a whole lot of dress missing in the back. She could only hope that the heating would be turned up in the ballroom.

"I like sequins," she said. "They're very glamorous. That doesn't mean they should be arranged into the shape of a fish and worn on some poor woman's chest."

"I'll never understand," Scott said as he moved to the dresser, then returned and handed her the little Christmas tree tiepin she'd given him.

It might have been after Christmas, but with her wearing her snowflake necklace, it seemed right that he wore her gift too. She attached the pin, then turned and picked up her wrap and clutch purse.

"Is it too late to cancel?" Scott said as he pulled her into his arms. He ran his hands down her bare back until they came to rest where the dress draped across the top of her bottom. When his hand slid inside, a shiver ran up her spine, followed by a flush of heat.

"Rain check?" she asked as she raised her lips to his for a short kiss that quickly became hot and demanding.

"I can think of so many ways to get you out of that dress," he said as he walked her back toward the bed.

Turning quickly, she ducked under his arm and headed for the front door. She'd almost made it when his arms caught her and pulled her back against him. "I'll give you until midnight. Then that dress is coming off. For both our sakes, let's hope we escape this party before the ball drops. Otherwise we're going to shock more than the granny panties off poor Ms. Connors."

When they stepped into the ballroom, Felicity was surprised at the number of people she recognized. There were senators and business moguls that she had seen on news reports on television, along with actors and actresses she had never dreamed of meeting.

"Are you sure this is the right place?" she asked as she took a glass of champagne from a waiter.

"Our names were on the guest list, so I'm thinking it has to be," Scott said as he took his own glass from the waiter. "There's no way they would have missed us if we hadn't shown up."

"Don't be so sure. I see Dr. Mason heading our way," she said.

"There you are, Scott. And, Felicity, you look lovely this evening. I'm so glad you could make it. And I know you'll have a lovely evening. Mr. Bernhardt always throws the best parties. He's been throwing a New Year's Eve party for as long as I've been at Brooklyn Heights. Most of the board members are here with their spouses, and of course there are a lot of people who have made donations to the hospital this year," Dr. Mason said as he looked around the room. "There he is. Do you mind if I borrow Scott for just a minute?"

She watched as Scott was dragged away to meet a nice-looking older man who seemed to be holding court in the middle of the ballroom. She had met most of the board members, but she didn't recognize this particular one.

While she waited for Scott, she wandered over to where a buffet had been set up. She had to admit that Dr. Mason was right. Mr. Bernhardt did throw a nice party. Pulling her phone out, she searched for their distinguished host and was surprised to find he was a self-made billionaire who had earned his fortune in construction.

"I feel like a trick pony," Scott said when he joined her.

"Really, what tricks do you do?" she asked.

"Ha ha," Scott said as he picked up a small cracker and popped it into his mouth. "At least I'm getting some treats."

"I don't know if he's showing you off or if he's courting you," she said as they began to move around the room, making a game out of seeing how many celebrities they each could find.

"Maybe," Scott said.

"I can't wait till I can call my mom tomorrow and tell her about all the people we've seen tonight."

"Can we leave yet? I'm pretty sure Dr. Mason has forgotten all about us," Scott said as he looked down at his watch.

"And take me home without even one dance on New Year's Eve?" she asked as she took his arm. "What kind of date are you?"

"A date that wants to be alone with you." He tapped the face of his watch before he pulled her into his arms. "We have less than two hours till midnight."

For the next hour, as the room buzzed with conversations that would be spread across the tabloids the next day and million-dollar deals were formed, the two of them danced as if they were the only two people in the room. And as far as Scott and Felicity were concerned, they were.

They made it back inside her apartment with fifteen minutes to spare. Her dress now lay puddled on the floor at the front door, along with his jacket and tie. She'd stripped him of his white shirt in the dining room. His pants lay in the doorway.

"If I'd known you had nothing on under that dress, we never would have made it out of the bedroom," he said as he kissed his way down her chest.

"I had on a thong," she said, then moaned when he took one of her nipples into his mouth and sucked it.

She gripped his back and knew tomorrow he would find where she had marked him with her little love scratches. His hand moved between her legs and she arched her body against his talented fingers.

"Yes, there," she moaned as she covered his neck with her kisses. He knew her body so well, touching her in just the right spot at the exact, perfect time. But then he had always known what she needed and when. It was his superpower.

His fingers became more insistent and his thrusts more demanding. He filled her up until she overflowed with a pleasure that consumed her, body and soul. She had been so empty before, but as pleasure overwhelmed her, it was too much to contain. She anchored herself to him with her arms and her legs. She wouldn't let go. She needed him too much. She screamed his name as wave after wave of pleasure rolled through her.

As the sound of "Auld Lang Syne" filled the room, Scott followed her into the New Year.

He woke her up later with soft kisses trailing down her spine, before he flipped her over onto her back. Their lovemaking was slow and easy this time, with intimate touches and kisses that soothed rather than excited. When he entered her, she wrapped her arms around him and pulled him down on top of her. She needed to feel every part of him against her. As they slowly moved together, she knew she would never be loved by another man like this one. It was as if they had been made to fit perfectly together. They matched each stroke, until their bodies gave way to a warm pleasure that was just as satisfying as the demanding lovemaking they had shared earlier that night.

As she dozed off to sleep, she rested her head against Scott's chest and listened to the strong, steady beat of his heart while tears ran down her cheeks. Only here in the dark, while he slept beneath her, could she admit how much she was going to miss this…miss him. In a day he would be gone and she would be left with the memories of their time together here in her apartment. Would they haunt her the same way her memories of Leo did?

How was she to go on alone after all they had shared? How was she supposed to learn to settle for the life she'd had before Scott had returned to New York? She knew things wouldn't go back to the way they'd been before. Even though things had changed after they'd become sexually involved, they still had a friendship that neither one could deny.

When sleep finally pulled her under, she dreamed of ballrooms and dances with princes, but then the clock would sound that

it was midnight and suddenly she found herself back in her apartment and her Prince
Charming was nowhere in sight.

CHAPTER THIRTEEN

"FLISS, WAKE UP," Scott said as he gently shook her. There was no reason to make this any harder than it was going to be by startling her out of sleep. "Honey, you have to wake up now."

Sleepy blue eyes blinked open, and his heart dropped into his stomach. He didn't want to be the person who had to do this. Not again. Hadn't she lost enough already? Hadn't they both? Would it be too much to ask to have everything go right for one more day?

He thought of the small jewelry box he had tucked into his suit pocket the night before. He should have shown it to her last night.

And he was a selfish jerk thinking of his own happiness right now.

"Honey, I need you to sit up and listen to

me." Scott moved over so she could reposition herself.

"What's wrong?" she asked, her voice still hoarse from sleep, her innocent eyes still foggy.

There was no way to say this without her panicking, he knew that, but he wanted to avoid it as much as possible. "Your mother just called. They've taken your father to the hospital."

"What?" she asked as she moved away from him. "What's wrong with him? Is it his stomach again?"

"No, honey, the doctor in the emergency room at home says it's an MI. They're going to take him to the cath lab." He watched as her face went pale. "I told them we would meet them at the hospital."

"We have to go. I need to be there. I should have been there," Felicity said as she jumped off the bed and headed to the bathroom, shutting the door behind her.

He waited outside the door, ready to step in if she sounded like she needed him. When she opened the door, her face had more color, but her eyes had lost the sparkle from the night before.

It took only minutes for the two of them to dress and pack a bag. Not knowing what they would find when they arrived at the hospital, they wanted to be prepared.

"When exactly did my mom call?" Felicity asked him as they buckled their seat belts.

He pulled out of the parking place and was happy to see that traffic was light. Most people were still in bed, sleeping off all the celebrating they had done the night before. "About two or three minutes before I woke you." He looked down at his watch. "About thirty minutes ago. She said she'd call back as soon as she knew something. I told her to call my cell phone."

"She called my phone," she said. "You answered my phone?"

"You were asleep. I thought it was probably the hospital. When I saw it was your mom…" He didn't have to say any more.

"And now she knows we're sleeping together. What if she tells your mother?" she said.

"If? My parents were at the hospital with her. I'm sure my mother has already been told," he said. And was that such a bad thing? Their parents were smart people. He'd be surprised if they hadn't already figured out something was going on between them.

"It doesn't matter now. The only thing that matters is my father," she said, though it seemed she was talking more to herself than to him.

Glancing over at her, Scott saw that she was staring at the phone she had clutched in her hand. "Call her. Maybe she has some news."

She hesitated for just a moment, then made the call. From the side of the conversation he could hear, it seemed her father was still in the cath lab.

"It's okay," Scott said when she hung up the phone. "You know sometimes these cases take a while. They would have informed your mother if there had been a change."

He went to take her hand, but she had turned away from him to look out the window. A chill that had nothing to do with the upstate New York winter seeped into his heart. Was he losing her again? He knew this would be a setback to the plans he had begun to make, but he wasn't going to give up on them again. There had to be a way to make things work between them.

He thought about the conversations he'd had with Dr. Mason over the last week and the night before at the party. It was a long shot, but he'd take it.

"I need to call London and let them know I won't be coming back tomorrow," he said.

"Can you do that?" she asked as she turned back to him. "You have a contract with them."

"Someone can cover for me. They'll understand. I won't leave until we know your father is going to be okay," he said.

"He has to be okay," she said as she turned back toward the window. "I should have been there."

"You can't stand guard over them, Fliss," he told her. "You have to live your own life."

"You don't understand. I wasn't here when Leo needed me. If I'd been here, things would have been different," she said.

"Do you really believe that?" He was tired of hearing her blame herself for something she had no part in. "You think just your presence would have made the difference in his life?"

"It could have. I would have seen that something was wrong if I'd been there."

"Like your parents saw it? Like the teachers he worked with saw it? No, Fliss, if Leo hadn't wanted you to know how bad things were for him, you never would have known either way. He had a mental disorder that he hid from everyone. You can't live the rest of your life carrying the responsibility of his death."

"You can't understand," she said, her voice lifeless now. Where had the woman he had held in his arms this morning gone?

"Why not? Because I've never lost anyone?

I lost my best friend. And then I lost you because of this crazy responsibility that you think you have to make sure you take care of everyone else." He tried to keep his voice down, but the emotions he had kept bottled up seemed to have taken over. "You didn't even give me the choice of staying here with you."

"And if I had?" she said as she turned to him, her eyes now sparking with anger. "Were you going to throw away all the work you had done to get the job in London for me? And what for? Because you'd slept with me once?"

"It could have been more than that, Fliss, and you know that." He made himself ignore the pain he felt at her words. She was upset about her father.

"It doesn't matter now. Your life is in London and mine is here in the States. What we've had here has been great, but we both knew it was only temporary."

He felt her withdrawal from him as she turned back to the window, taking away any hope that he'd had for a future together.

* * *

By the time they pulled into the hospital parking lot, it had been almost three hours since her mother's first call. She'd called to tell them Fliss's father was out of the cath lab, but he'd been taken to the cardiovascular intensive care unit and they had not been allowed back yet.

"Why haven't they let Mom back to see him? We always get the family back with their patient," Felicity said as they rushed into the hospital.

They found her mom in the waiting room, along with Scott's parents. A tall man in a white lab coat that she didn't recognize sat beside them.

"Fliss, I'm so glad you're here," her mother said after they exchanged a tight hug. "This is Dr. Nelson. He's the doctor that performed the heart cath on your father."

"It's nice to meet you. Your mother says you work at Brooklyn Heights in New York in their cardiac unit," the doctor said.

"Yes, I do. And this is Dr. Thomas. He's

a cardiologist temporarily here from London," she said, then got down to business. She didn't have time for these unnecessary pleasantries. "What did you find when you did the heart cath on my father?"

"I was just telling your mother that your father is stable for the moment. We put in a stent, but his left main artery is significantly blocked. The bottom line is that he needs open-heart surgery and the sooner the better," the doctor said. Standing, he turned to Scott. "I can show you the scans if you would like."

"If it's okay with everyone." Scott turned and looked at her and her mother. They both nodded their agreement.

Felicity would have liked to have seen the scans herself, but she knew Scott was the professional who had more experience in the cath lab. Besides, it was likely that her father's doctor would talk more openly with another doctor.

"Good. I'm available right now if that's okay with you," Dr. Nelson said. "And if the rest of you will remain here, I'll let the staff know that they can take you back to see Mr. Dale."

Felicity watched as the doctor and Scott walked off together. She'd felt almost numb for the last three hours, but now all the panic she had been able to hold back wanted to rush through her. Her daddy needed open-heart surgery.

"I should have made him go to the emergency room on Christmas Day," she said aloud, finally voicing the thought that had haunted her since she'd first heard about her father's heart attack. If she'd had him checked out, all of this might have been avoided.

"This wasn't the same, Fliss. He woke me up and told me that this was something different. The pain was different. That other pain, it does make him feel sick and it does give him some bad nights with reflux, but this was different," her mother said as she put her arm around her daughter. "It's going to be okay. The doctor was telling us before you got here that he should recover within weeks of the surgery."

Felicity knew that open-heart surgery was very common. She worked with patients who had the surgery and recovered without any complications all the time. But this was different. This was her father.

A nurse came to get her mother and take her to the intensive care unit to see her husband. Felicity quietly sat in her seat and waited her turn.

Had it only been a year and a half since she had sat in a waiting room much like this one? Her brother had been declared brain dead as soon as he had arrived at the hospital, but he had remained on life support until her parents had accepted that he wouldn't be coming back to them. After agreeing to organ donation, she had waited with her parents for a nurse to come and tell her that her brother was truly gone. His organs had been harvested and she knew his heart had been given to another young man not much older than her brother.

"What did you find out?" she said, jumping out of her seat as Scott came back into the room.

"Dr. Nelson is a sharp man. He's right. Your father's left main has a large block. I'd suggest he goes to open-heart as soon as possible too." Scott reached out and took her hand. Unable to help herself, she let him pull her into his arms. It wasn't like they had anything to hide from their parents now.

"I want him transferred to Brooklyn Heights," she said against his shoulder.

"I told him you would say that. As long as your mother agrees, he will get it arranged." Scott held on to her as they joined his parents.

When her mother returned, she explained how to find the unit and Felicity made her way to her father's room.

"Daddy?" she said as she walked over to his bed. When his eyes opened, she felt some of the fear leave her. "How are you doing?"

"I'm fine, baby girl. I just need a little rest and I'll be right back to normal." His smile was weak, but she was glad to see that he was in good spirits, though some of that might have been from the meds he'd been given.

Her mother had asked her to be the one to tell him that he was going to need another surgery. She took a deep breath. She'd gotten her stubbornness from her father. If she didn't phrase this exactly right, he would likely give them problems. Not that it was an option. He would have the surgery no matter what. There wasn't a choice at this point.

"I met your doctor, Dr. Nelson. He seems to know what he's talking about and he let Scott take a look at the films they made during your heart catheterization when they put the stent in."

"I only got one stent? My boss at work— you know Mr. Stone—he got three of those stents and he was back at work in no time." Her father reached out his hand to her. "I'm going to be okay. Don't you worry."

"It's not just the stent, Daddy. It's more than that. Scott and Dr. Nelson saw a large blockage to your left main artery and it's preventing the blood from reaching your heart. You need to have open-heart surgery and they want to do it as soon as possible." She waited for her father to say something, to try to blow this off as something that wasn't that serious, but he only looked down where he held her hand.

"You think I need to have this done?" he asked, his voice almost too soft to hear with all the noise from the machines and pumps in the room.

"I do. And I want you to come to Brooklyn Heights to have it done," she said. The fact that he wasn't arguing with her told her that the chest pain he'd had before he came to the emergency room had been bad.

"Can you send Scott in to see me, please?" he said as he let go of her hand. "I'd like to talk to him for a few minutes."

She kissed his cheek, then headed back to the waiting room, where her mother stood talking to some of her father's coworkers who had come in while she had been with her dad.

"He wants to talk to you," she told Scott. "He's taking things better than I thought. He didn't try to play things down or try to argue with me. I think he just needs to hear from you that he needs the surgery."

She walked together with him to the unit, then waited for him outside the doors. The lack of sleep from the night before and the stress of the day were beginning to wear her down. She leaned against the wall and closed her eyes. A few minutes later the doors to the unit opened and Scott walked out, wearing a smile.

"Did things go that well?" she asked when they started back to the waiting room.

"What do you mean?" Scott asked.

"You're smiling. He must have agreed to the surgery and the transfer, right?" she asked.

"Oh, yes, he agreed. I'm going to call Dr. Nelson as soon as we get back to the waiting room." He took her hand as they walked back to join the others. "Why don't you go close your eyes for a few minutes? I'll make the phone call and start making some arrangements in New York."

She was too tired to argue. She took a seat

next to Scott's dad, who had found a magazine to read, and she shut her eyes, only to have them open again when Scott took the seat next to her. "Back so soon?" she asked.

"I was gone at least thirty minutes," he said.

She could tell that the lack of sleep was catching up to him too.

"Where's my mom?" she asked as she sat up and looked around the room.

"She's with your father," Scott's father said as he looked up from his magazine.

A few minutes later, when her mom and Dr. Nelson walked into the room together, she stood. There was something about the way the doctor was bending over her mother, comforting her, that told Felicity there had been a change.

"It's okay, Fliss. Your father's just having more chest pain," her mom said as she tried to reassure her. "Dr. Nelson was telling me that if we're going to transfer your father, we need to do it now, before it becomes an emergency situation."

"I just got off the phone with the doctor on

call at Brooklyn and he's just waiting for your call, Dr. Nelson. He assures me there will be a bed available within the hour and he can call in the surgical team as soon as Mr. Dale arrives," Scott said. He rested his hands on her shoulders. "Brooklyn has offered their helicopter service for transport if you don't have it available."

"I'll call our transfer center and the doctor now," Dr. Nelson said before leaving the room.

"I can't thank you enough, Scott, for helping us," her mother told him as she leaned over and kissed him on the cheek.

Finally the word came that the helicopter would be there within the hour. It wasn't until she and Scott were in the car and headed back to New York that she realized what was supposed to be Scott's final day in New York was almost over. He'd been so busy. Had he had a chance to call London? But she couldn't think about that now. She was already too close to falling apart, and she needed to be strong for her mother. She had to make sure her father was going to be okay. That was what was important right now. Everything else would have to wait.

The sun had set before they arrived back in New York and the nighttime traffic was heavy as they slowly made their way to the hospital. He'd let Felicity sleep during their ride back to the city.

"Wake up, sleepyhead," he said as he nudged her awake. "We're almost there."

"Has the hospital called?" she asked as she sat up. Her face was marked with wrinkles from where she had leaned against the seat, and her hair had come down from the twisty knot she had wrapped it in that morning.

"I received a text less than an hour ago from Dr. Mason, who said your father had arrived safely and was being prepped for surgery." He wasn't going to tell her about the other part of the doctor's message. Dr. Mason had been very specific that he didn't want anyone to know about the negotiations he was in with the Royal Kensington Hospital to extend Scott's time in Brooklyn Heights. So far there had been no response from the London hospital and it had been arranged for him to leave the next evening.

"Where's Mom and your parents?" she asked as she turned to look at the traffic behind them.

"They're not far behind." He parked his car and they made their way into the hospital and up to the cardiac floor.

"Let me find out where they took him while you wait for your parents. From what Dr. Mason said, they were already getting his lines put in for the surgery, so he's probably already been taken to pre-op," Felicity said and then headed down the hall and through a door that said Staff Only.

Fifteen minutes later she returned looking more pale and tired than she had before. "They've already taken him to surgery. They said he became short of breath and Dr. Hyland felt he needed to go to surgery right away."

"George Hyland is a very good cardiothoracic surgeon. Your father is in good hands. You know that," Scott said as he took her hands in his.

"You know we say those words to people all the time, but on this side of things, it doesn't seem to help. I just wish I'd been able to see him before they took him in for surgery. What if...?"

"There are no what-ifs here. Your father is a healthy man. There's no reason for us to think he's not going to do well in the operating room. We just have to be patient," Scott said. The waiting room was empty, as being a holiday, there were no scheduled surgeries. Taking a seat in a corner of the room, they prepared themselves to wait. He thought about the plans he'd had to talk to Felicity today about their future.

This was not the place to do this. But what choice did he really have? He'd been given a few extra days, but as soon as Fliss's father got through recovery, they were expecting him to return. Thinking about heading back to London should have excited him. He did love his job there and it was the job he had dreamed of for years. But he'd learned over the last year and a half that without the woman he loved beside him, he would never be happy.

"You know…" he started, then stopped when he saw his parents and Felicity's mom.

"Have you seen him?" Felicity's mom asked them.

"They've already taken him into surgery," Felicity said, then explained that her father's condition had deteriorated and the doctor had felt he needed to start before they arrived.

"I was about to go to the OR and make sure they knew we were here," Felicity said as she started to stand.

"Let me go. The last thing we need is a turf war between you and the OR staff," Scott said as he stood and stretched his legs. "I'll be back in a few minutes."

But he didn't go right back. After checking in with the OR and finding that there was nothing new to report back to Felicity and her mom, he wandered back through the hospital to the office he had been using in the cardiac center and started making some phone calls.

CHAPTER FOURTEEN

FELICITY STOOD IN the doorway of her father's intensive care bed and watched him sleep. Scott had been right. Her father was a healthy man and the surgery had been declared a success. After a few weeks of recovery time, he'd be right back to work.

Scott had arranged for rooms for both his parents and her mother at a hotel only a block from the hospital. At some point Scott had disappeared and she assumed he had found an empty doctor's sleep room.

"Ow," her father moaned as he tried to turn in the bed.

"Daddy, don't," she said as she rushed into the room. "You're attached to a bunch of lines that could get pulled out."

"Fliss?" he asked. He still looked weak, but color had returned to his face, and with the smile he always had for her, he at least resembled her father.

"Yeah, it's me. You had surgery. Do you remember?" she asked as she sat down in the small plastic chair beside his bed.

"Of course I remember. I remember the trip in that helicopter too. I'd rather not repeat that one," he said. "Where's your mother? Is she doing okay?"

"She's at a hotel down the street. Scott pulled some strings and got her a last-minute room." She adjusted the sheets around her father.

"That Scott is a good man. You won't find better," her father said. "Did he tell you about our conversation?"

"About the surgery?" she asked.

"No. I didn't need him to tell me about the surgery. If you thought I needed the surgery, that was enough for me." Her father tried to turn toward her.

"Let me help," she said as she guarded the lines, then assisted him to roll onto his side. "Better?"

"Much better. This bed is as hard as a concrete bench," he said. "Look, I know me and your mom should stay out of your life…but I think we need to talk."

"Maybe this should wait till later, when you feel better," she said.

"No, this can't be put off," her father said. The monitor above his bed alarmed, showing that his heart rate had increased.

"It's okay, Daddy. I didn't mean to upset you," she said.

"No, I did it myself. I should have said this earlier, and now with things the way they are with you and Scott… We didn't say anything after Leo died and you decided to move back home. And I'm sorry about that. At the time, it seemed that you needed to be here and we sure needed you. But now, looking back, it was a mistake…"

"No, it wasn't, Daddy. I needed to be here with you," she said as she moved closer to her dad. "You need to rest now."

"No, baby girl. There's still things I need to say. It was a mistake for us to let you give up the life you had made in London. And then there's Scott. We knew there was something wrong when you avoided talking about him, but we didn't know... Well, maybe at some point we had hoped... But I can see it now. You gave up Scott to come home for us," her father said, then pinned her with a look that wouldn't let her be anything but honest with him.

"It was nothing, really. We'd just started to see each other, that way," she said. She looked up at the monitors and pretended to study them.

"And now?" her father asked her. "Don't bother denying that you two are involved. I've already talked to Scott."

"Daddy, you know Scott's life is in London and mine is here," she said as she stood up and stepped away from the bed. This was exactly what she had feared would happen when her mother found out she and Scott were involved.

"Why?" her father asked.

"Why? Because Scott loves his job and I love you and Mom. Look at today. What would have happened if I hadn't been here with you?" She made herself calm down. She wouldn't upset her dad no matter how hard this was for her.

"I suspect I would have had the surgery and you would have caught a plane as soon as possible so that you could be here to hover over me like you're doing now," he said as he reached out to her.

"I'm sorry. I don't mean to hover. It's just that I love you and Mom so much. I don't want to lose you. Not like I lost Leo. If I'd been here, then…"

Her father squeezed her hand. "I was here, Fliss, and I couldn't stop what happened to your brother. If you're to blame, your mother and I are even more to blame."

"No, Daddy, it wasn't your fault," she said, moving closer to his bed.

"And it wasn't yours either. You can't stop living because of some misplaced guilt you feel about your brother's death, honey. You have to move on now. Life's hard. Everyone needs someone in their life they can count on, someone who will always be there for them. For me, that's your mom. I think Scott could be that person for you, if you'll let him." Her father closed his eyes. Their conversation had worn him out.

In a few minutes, his breathing became even and she slipped out of the room. After making sure that the nurses had her phone number, she left the unit. She started to go back to the waiting room, but after the last twenty-four hours, she needed a change.

She stepped out of the front entrance of the hospital and onto a sidewalk that was covered in the slush that had been yesterday's snow. As the cold air rushed through her lungs, she pulled her coat around her, then walked across the street to a small all-night diner.

She had ordered a cup of coffee and a cinnamon roll to keep her going when her phone sounded with a text from Scott. After giving him her location, she ordered another cup of coffee. Her father had been right about many things. She had spent the last year and a half trying to be the perfect daughter who was always there for her parents when the truth was that her parents didn't need her. Not that they didn't love her. She had no doubt they loved her.

But after Leo died, she'd let her pain and guilt drive her into thinking that she needed to always be close to her parents so she could keep them safe. She wouldn't let them down like she had let Leo down.

Scott took the seat across from her and picked up the coffee she'd ordered for him.

"Do you know why I moved out of my parents' house and went to the city?" she asked him.

"You said you were bored at the hospital in Hudson." He took a sip of the coffee.

"I was, but I would have stayed there anyway to be close to my parents. No, the reason I moved out was because my mom told me I needed to get a place of my own. She said I was cramping their style."

Scott choked on his laughter as his coffee splashed against the table. "Really?"

"I know. Sad, right? My parents have more

of a life than I do." She set her coffee down. No matter what happened next, she needed to say this. "I'm sorry for how I ended things after Leo died. I don't expect you to understand, but I couldn't have gone back to London. Not then. No matter how strong my parents might be now, they needed me then. And I needed them too. But ending our friendship like that was wrong."

"And now? What is it you want now?" he asked, his eyes intense as he studied her.

And that was the million-dollar question, wasn't it? But she knew what she wanted. She wanted it all. She wanted what she had with Scott now, but she also wanted more. She wanted the kind of love her parents had. She wanted to know that the person she loved would always be there for her, just like she would always be there for him.

"I want a friend," she said as she looked up from her coffee.

"I'll be that friend," he said, never taking his eyes off her.

"I want a lover," she said as she moved her hand over to where his rested on the table.

"I'll be that lover," he said as he joined their hands.

"I want a father for our children," she said. She brushed her tears away with her free hand.

"I'll be that father, Fliss," he said as he lifted her hand to his mouth.

"Okay," she said, then giggled. "Did I just ask you to marry me, Scott Thomas?"

"I think you did," he said as he leaned across the table to kiss her. "You wouldn't happen to have a ring with you, would you?"

"No, I'm afraid I didn't see far enough ahead to bring a ring," she said as she wiped more tears away. While she had dreamed of being Mrs. Scott Thomas most of her life, she'd never imagined she would be the one to propose to him.

"Well, I guess it's a good thing that I thought far enough ahead for the two of us," he said as he pulled a jewelry box from his jacket pocket and placed it on the faded laminate tabletop.

Opening the box, he revealed the most beautiful ring she had ever seen. And as he slipped the ring onto her finger, in an all-night diner in the middle of the night, Dr. Scott Thomas made all of Felicity's childhood dreams come true.

EPILOGUE

SHE RECOGNIZED HIM the minute she walked into the room. That head of dark hair that she loved to run her fingers through, those wide shoulders that she knew she could count on to hold her up when things went wrong and that perfectly tailored tux that she had finally gotten him into were enough to assure her that this was the man she was looking for.

The organ began to play and he turned toward her, smiling in the way that had always sent butterflies racing through her stomach, and suddenly they were the only two people in the cathedral.

"Ready?" her father asked her.

She stared back at the man who stood at the altar waiting for her. Ready? For this? For him?

"I've never been more ready," she replied

as she took that first step that would begin the rest of her life.

Later, when the vows had been said and the cake had been cut, they left the dancing couples and sneaked away to a small alcove where the two of them could be alone.

"So what is this surprise you have for me?" Felicity asked as she looked around.

"I've spoken to our parents and they've all agreed to come over to London for Christmas. I gave them the tickets right before the wedding," Scott said.

Throwing her arms around him, she kissed him. "Thank you so much. I can't wait. We'll have to take them shopping in Covent Garden. And we can go to that cute little market and get a tree. I've already shipped the snowflake ornaments, but we'll want a bigger tree for your place, so we'll need to order more. I hope—"

"We have six months till Christmas. Why don't we get through the honeymoon and get moved back before we start decorating?" Scott said as he fingered the small snowflake necklace she had insisted on wearing, even though it was a June wedding.

"I know. And there's going to be so much for you to get caught up on at work. A lot of things have probably changed in the last six months," she said. The fact that he'd arranged to have his contract extended so he could remain with her while her father recovered and while she and their mothers planned the wedding was a true testament to his love for her. "And there'll be even more for me to catch up on in the cath lab there."

"And I still don't know where we're going on our honeymoon," he said.

She'd had to work to get him to agree that since she had done the proposing, she should get to plan the honeymoon. She knew he was going to love the cabin she had rented in the Catskill Mountains where they could hike and fish all day and then spend long nights in an isolated paradise.

"It's tradition that the honeymoon is a surprise. Can't you wait just a little longer?" she asked as they made their way back to their reception.

"For you, Fliss, I would wait a lifetime."

* * * * *

LET'S TALK

Romance

For exclusive extracts, competitions
and special offers, find us online:

f facebook.com/millsandboon

⊙ @millsandboonuk

🐦 @millsandboon

Or get in touch on 0844 844 1351*

For all the latest titles coming soon,
visit millsandboon.co.uk/nextmonth